RESCUED

HOLT AGENCY, BOOK ONE

BECCA JAMESON

Copyright © 2022 by Becca Jameson

Cover Artist: Original Syn

All characters and events in this book are fictitious. And resemblance to actual persons living or dead is strictly coincidental.

All rights reserved.

No part of this book may be reproduced in any form or by any electronic or mechanical means, including information storage and retrieval systems, without written permission from the author, except for the use of brief quotations in a book review.

❦ Created with Vellum

ACKNOWLEDGMENTS

I'd like to thank my family for all their help with this book. We all traveled to Uganda together, but their memories are better than mine! Without them, I wouldn't have been able to get all the details correct.

Scott, Rebecca, and James, you are the best! Love you!

LETTER TO THE READER

Dear readers,

KaLyn Cooper and I are very excited to bring you this new collaborative series, the Holt Agency. If you're a fan of the Shadow SEALs books, you might remember us introducing this agency in each of our first two releases. The men who open the Holt Agency were all rescued SEALs who appeared in *Shadow in the Desert* and *Shadow in the Mountain*. The following year, several characters were once again featured in *Shadow in the Darkness* and *Shadow in the Daylight*.

So, welcome to the Holt Agency! The headquarters is located at a farm in Indiana. The former SEALs who have joined forces and opened the agency will each get their own happily ever afters in the coming books.

Rescued
Unchained

Protected
Liberated
Defended
Unrestrained

CHAPTER 1

"Where are you exactly?"

Tavis inhaled slowly, not liking the sound of Ajax's voice, or his word choice. "Entebbe International Airport. But you knew this. What's up?"

"Perfect. Change of plans. Don't board the plane."

Tavis sighed as he dropped onto a cold vinyl airport seat and rubbed his forehead. "You've got another rescue mission that happens to be in Uganda?" He'd just finished locating a college student who had stopped answering his parents' calls. His wealthy parents. Parents who really needed to stop funding their kid's world tour until he was mature enough to touch base with his family more frequently.

The kid had been fine. Drunk. Partying. Spending Daddy's money without a care in the world. Tavis hated this kind of job. There were plenty of legitimately missing people in the world who really needed rescuing. Rich spoiled college boys weren't among them.

But that had been the job, and who was Tavis to judge what wealthy people wanted to spend their money on?

"It's not a rescue per se," his boss at the Holt Agency informed him from their home base on his foster parents' farm in Indiana.

When Ajax and Ryker formed the Holt Agency a year ago, they'd hired the rest of their now retired SEAL team to join them. Their clients were often private citizens or government officials who needed someone found, rescued, or protected, but Tavis preferred not being assigned to protection detail. There were far better ways to use his skills.

Tavis leaned back in his chair and stared at the ceiling. "As long as it isn't another frat boy needing a babysitter."

Ajax chuckled, but his voice lacked humor.

"Ajax…" Tavis warned. "Toss me something worthwhile. Something humanitarian. Something that helps the planet. Someone deserving of rescue."

"Sorry, Bones." No one had called him by his SEAL nickname since he'd officially left the Navy after being held captive by Ethiopian rebels. Since Ajax had rescued him and the rest of their platoon, he'd let the man call him anything he wanted. "But hey, it's not a college boy this time."

"Thank God."

"It's a college girl."

Tavis groaned. "Why on earth do all these rich people let their irresponsible children travel to third-world countries? Do they lack common sense?"

"This case is different. And the college student is actually a PhD candidate. She's not a girl. She's a woman. And she's not missing. She's on her way there."

Tavis drew in a breath. "Then why do you need me?"

"Because her father is the secretary of state, and he wants her to have a bodyguard."

Tavis swallowed. "*The* secretary of state? You mean William Loughlin?"

"That's the one."

"I didn't even know he *had* a daughter."

"Yeah, well, he does."

"How old is she?"

"Twenty-seven. Harvard graduate. Working on her doctorate in epidemiology from Johns Hopkins."

"Fuck me," Tavis muttered under his breath. *She's an epidemiologist?* "Shit."

"Yeah."

"What do you need me for? Is she already in trouble?"

"Her father wants her to have protection."

Tavis's eyebrows rose. "Against what?"

"No idea. He seems overprotective. He's assigned personal bodyguards to her for years."

Tavis groaned. "I'm not a bodyguard. I find people. Rescue them. Since when are we in the habit of prevention instead of intervention?"

"I know. But he's desperate."

"Why is he desperate?" Something about this assignment felt off.

"Ryker has done most of the communicating with Secretary Loughlin, but I get the feeling she's difficult."

Tavis groaned louder. "Ajax…"

"I know. I know. But the money is good. Amazing. And the job is easy. Just keep an eye on the ornery student."

"And how long is this assignment?"

Tavis could hear Ajax wince.

"Ajax…"

"You're the best person for this assignment because you're already there," Ajax stated, not even beginning to answer the question.

"And I'm single. And I don't have kids." He wasn't the

only single guy with no kids at the Holt Agency. But he was one of the few who didn't have much family.

"I didn't say that."

"Yeah, yeah. Whatever. You didn't answer my question."

"Six months."

Tavis drew in a breath. He'd envisioned a week on the beach in Florida and then maybe a local assignment somewhere at least in North America this time. Six months in Uganda?

Frankly, Tavis would rather be assigned to something a bit more exciting than bodyguard, but he realized there were often underlying issues with any job. If the secretary of state needed a man on his daughter, there could be more going on than Ajax was aware of.

Tavis sighed and ran his hand down his face. "When does she arrive?"

"Tomorrow. Midnight. Coming in from Amsterdam through Rwanda."

"Yeah, I know the flight." Another inhale. Another exhale. So much for a week in Florida. "I'll be here." He shoved to standing and headed toward the desk where he'd just checked into his flight so he could cancel.

"Thanks, man. I promise, the next job will be cushy after a long vacation."

"Sure. I'll believe that when it happens," Tavis joked.

"I'll email you the details in a few minutes. Touch base when you can."

"Will do." Tavis pocketed his phone and shuffled reluctantly to the counter. Great. Just great. This wasn't some rich family's irresponsible kid. This was a very important family's grown-ass daughter.

Six months was a long time. Tavis prayed the woman wasn't a bitch. That would make the time drag on forever.

CHAPTER 2

Colette was still nursing a hangover when the plane landed in Entebbe. She'd been traveling for almost thirty hours, but not long enough to erase her poor judgment from the night before. At least she was no longer nauseous. All she had left was the lingering headache and a bad mood.

Why on earth had she let her friends talk her into going out on her last night in the States? It was so unlike her. She never drank like that. She never partied like that. She shuddered. There were a lot of things from that night she never did.

She groaned as she grabbed her bag from the overhead compartment, remembering why she'd been so damn foolish. She'd been furious with her parents. She was a grown woman, for God's sake. She didn't need a bodyguard while working in Uganda.

Besides the fact that they'd gone behind her back to arrange for her to have fulltime protection from their imaginary foes, they'd intentionally not informed her of their decision until the last minute.

That was what had fueled her to go out and get drunk.

Anger and frustration. How was anyone supposed to think of her as their equal in her field of study if she had a damn protection detail following her around?

He'd probably be some sort of bouncer type. Some buff guy with more muscles than brains. She pictured dark sunglasses, a crew cut, tattoos, and a fixed expression that never changed.

Would he be one of those guys whose arms didn't quite touch his torso because his biceps were too large for them to hang naturally?

She also knew from experience that a bodyguard had a tendency to make the people around her swoon. No one would look at her seriously because they'd be distracted by the man candy behind her.

This was the attitude she was carrying with her as she stepped off the plane.

Tired. Hungry. Aggravated. Still sporting a headache.

After working her way through customs and all the red tape involved with visas and immunization cards, she finally retrieved her bags and stepped outside into the pleasant night air.

One thing was for sure, the weather in Uganda was amazing year-round. She was looking forward to enjoying it.

It was nearly midnight and she was grouchy. She was also secretly a bit glad for the moment that her unwanted bodyguard would be picking her up. And doubly so when she spotted the man holding up a sign with her name on it.

Yep. He was all those things she'd visualized. He didn't have sunglasses on at this hour, but he did have short-cropped hair, several tattoos on his biceps, and a sour expression. If she wasn't mistaken, he was as excited about meeting her as she was him.

"I don't suppose you'd accept a wire transfer for twice

what my father paid you to pretend you did your job and leave me alone?" she stated by way of introduction as she approached him.

He slowly smirked, proving he could change his expression. "If it wouldn't get me fired, I'd take you up on that offer." He held out his hand. "Tavis Neade."

She reached out to shake his hand. "Colette Loughlin, but you already know that." His grip was firm. Everything about him was firm. As much as she wanted to hate him, it wasn't his fault he'd been hired to guard her. She shouldn't take it out on him.

"Yep. Did my research. You have an impressive resume." He glanced at her suitcase and then her backpack. "Is that all you have?"

She frowned at him. "Yes. Not all women travel with enough clothes and toiletries and shoes to blanket the earth. I'm a minimalist."

He smiled as he reached for the handle on her suitcase.

She swatted his hand away. "I've got it."

He lifted his brows, giving her another of his oddly sexy smirks. "Independent, huh?"

"Very."

"Well, let's assume my mother is looking down on me from heaven. Lightning will strike me if I let you pull your own suitcase to the car. You might actually get shocked by your proximity. So, let's not take the risk." He grabbed the handle and lifted the suitcase off the ground instead of pulling it, acting like it weighed nothing.

Colette jerked her gaze to his. "Sorry about your mom. How long has she been gone?"

"Ten years. Don't worry. Not a fresh wound. Let's go." He nodded toward the parking lot.

"I didn't realize how small this airport would be. And

how did you manage to park this close?" she asked as they reached the SUV ten seconds later.

"VIP parking. All I did was pay the guy at the gate a few shillings." He opened the back and tucked her suitcase in before rounding to the left side and opening the door for her. "Ready?"

Right. He's going to drive on the right side. She'd known that.

After he climbed behind the wheel, she glanced at him. "Why do you have such a serious vehicle? We planning to go off-roading?" she joked.

He chuckled. "You've never been to Uganda, have you?"

"No." She winced, hating that he knew things she didn't. She preferred to be the smartest in the room. And she usually was. She hadn't had a chance to do much research on this country or Kampala before arriving, and for that she figured she was about to experience some culture shock.

"Nearly everything is off-roading in Uganda. There aren't many paved roads. Most of the country is covered with clay-like soil, and it can be bumpy and rutted even in the city."

She looked out the window. "I suppose my father already told you where I'm staying. Please tell me we're going there now. I'm exhausted." She rubbed her temples, still fighting the headache. She needed a few painkillers and a good night's sleep.

"Yep. You can rest if you want. We'll be there in less than an hour."

She slumped in the seat, closing her eyes. For as much as she didn't want a bodyguard, she was grateful that she didn't have to figure out her own transportation this late at night or get a hotel nearby until tomorrow. There was plenty of time to make sure Tavis Neade understood how much she disliked him following her around later. After sleep.

It seemed like moments passed before Colette jolted awake when the SUV stopped. She'd been dead asleep.

"We're there, princess." Tavis jumped down from his side of the car and rounded to hers to open the door before she could formulate a response. But the moment he had her door open, she shot him a glare.

"Don't you dare call me that. I'm the least princess-like person you'll ever meet, and I hate the implication."

He chuckled. "I can see that. That's why I said it."

"To antagonize me? Why would you do that?"

He shrugged. "Because it was funny watching your feathers get ruffled."

She jumped down from her seat, still fuming as he grabbed her suitcase from the back of the SUV. He handed her the backpack next.

"Come on. You need more sleep."

She glanced up at the condo in front of them and hesitated. "This isn't the right address. I rented a fourth-floor apartment. The building was rust-colored in the pictures."

Tavis kept walking as he pulled a set of keys out of his pocket and then opened the ground-floor door in front of them. "I don't know anything about that. This is the address my boss gave me. I assume he got it from your father. I picked up the keys and stocked the fridge earlier today."

No. This couldn't be happening.

Colette stopped walking and stood frozen in her spot a few yards from the entrance. She rubbed her temples with both hands, furious with her father and his tendency to take over her life.

"Colette?"

She gritted her teeth to avoid screaming and stomping her foot. She hated being reduced to this level of anger that made her act like a damn child.

Tavis set her suitcase inside and turned back toward her. "Headache?"

"Understatement." She lifted her gaze. "Please tell me you're not staying here with me." She might turn around and get back on the next flight to the States to singlehandedly strangle her parents if they'd crossed that line.

Tavis winced. "No one filled you in on any of the details, did they?"

"Grrr." She was too fucking tired to deal with this man or anyone else. She stiffened her arms, fisted her hands, and stomped past him to enter the ridiculously nice furnished condo that her father had rented in an effort to interfere with and control every aspect of her life.

Tavis followed her inside, shut the door, and locked it.

"We sharing a bed too?" Colette asked as she glanced around the downstairs before grabbing her suitcase and lugging it up to the second floor where she assumed she would find two bedrooms. Her father was high-handed and domineering, but surely he didn't expect her to actually sleep with the bodyguard. Though, she wouldn't be surprised at this point.

"Seems like that might be unprofessional, but if you're afraid of the dark or have nightmares or something, I'll see what I can do to get you tucked back in. We could get a nightlight?"

Even though he couldn't see her face, she rolled her eyes and kept climbing the stairs.

"Master bedroom is on the right," he pointed out, reaching past her to push the door open. "I checked the mosquito net earlier. It's in good shape."

She avoided touching him as she entered and dropped her suitcase and backpack on the floor before sitting on the edge of the bed and pulling off her shoes.

She groaned as they hit the floor, and then she stood and pulled the covers back. "In about two seconds I'm going to strip down to my panties and climb under these covers. You going to watch or...?" She reached for the button on her jeans. At this point, she didn't give a fuck if he stayed or left. She just wanted to sleep.

Tavis chuckled as he rounded to the other side of the queen-sized bed and untied the netting from the bedpost. He did the same at the foot of the bed and then the corner closest to her before reaching around her to get the last one. "Make sure it falls shut around you, princess. Sleep tight."

She wanted to throw something at him as he left the room, but she inhaled slowly and blew it out just as slowly instead. She couldn't have hit him with anything anyway. She was trapped inside the mosquito netting.

Her fingers were shaking as she lowered the zipper on her jeans, shrugged out of them, and then removed her shirt, bra, and socks. In seconds she was in bed, under the covers, fast asleep.

CHAPTER 3

Tavis strolled back downstairs, snagged himself a bottle of water from the fridge, and dropped into the armchair in the living room. He pulled out his cell and called the Holt Agency headquarters in Indiana. It would be late afternoon there.

"Holt Agency." The pleasant friendly voice was that of Serena, Ajax's wife. She kept everything running like a well-oiled machine.

"Hey, Serena. This is Tavis. Is Ajax around?"

"Oh, hey, Tavis. He sure is. Hang on one second."

He knew she dashed into the other room to get her husband, knowing Tavis was calling from Uganda. Serena knew where every member of their team was at all times.

"Tavis, how's it going?"

Tavis laughed as he ran a hand over his short-cropped hair. "Depends on how you look at it."

"Please tell me you didn't have trouble picking her up from the airport."

"Oh, I found her easily. She's a spitfire. The last thing she wants is a bodyguard. She might have steamrolled right over me, left me on the side of the road, taken the keys to the SUV, and sped away if she weighed more than one twenty."

Ajax laughed. "I'd like to see something like that. Ryker told me he got the impression she wasn't exactly privy to some of the details."

"To be fair, Colette is a grown woman. Not a child. She isn't the sort of person who goes on drinking binges and gets into trouble. Her research is mostly in Kampala on the Makerere University campus. I'm sure she's brilliant and extremely capable and doesn't need a bodyguard. Unless there's something the secretary of state isn't telling us."

"Not that I'm aware of. But I'll dig around a bit."

"Has he always been this high handed with her?"

"I think so. She's an only child with a recognizable name. He's overprotective," Ajax pointed out.

"I could understand that if she were twelve or behaved badly."

"Funny you should mention that. Apparently she went out with her friends the night before she left and got a bit rowdy. There are pictures of her partying all over the internet today."

Tavis groaned. "You sure it was her? She doesn't seem the type." She did have a headache though. Could have been from drinking too much. Would also explain her sour disposition.

"Yep. Have her check in with her parents as soon as she can."

Tavis leaned his head back and stared at the ceiling. The perfect ceiling in this expensive, brand new, furnished condo. "I doubt if that would go over well. She doesn't strike me as someone who's going to enjoy being told what to do."

None of this made sense. There had to be a piece

missing from the story. The woman who just growled at him and nearly stripped in front of him indignantly did not strike him as someone who partied all night on a regular basis. Hell, she had an advanced degree in something medical he knew nothing about.

Suddenly, he decided he would open his laptop and educate himself before morning. If she thought he was some dumb bodyguard, he would prove her wrong and nip that in the bud and fast.

"You still there?" Ajax asked.

"Yeah. Can you dig around some and see if there's anything good ole Daddy isn't sharing with us? The hairs on the back of my neck are standing on end."

"Will do," Ajax responded. "I agree. Something doesn't add up."

"Maybe I'm overreacting and he's simply overprotective, but I suspect there's more to it than that. Either she's secretly a wild child on the side when not curing diseases—which I'm not buying—or there's a threat to her life no one bothered to mention."

"Agreed. I'm on it. Get some sleep. Sounds like you might need it."

"Will do." Tavis ended the call. He had no plans to sleep anytime soon though. He needed to know more about epidemiology and what sort of research studies were being conducted at Makerere University.

Why? So you can impress the lady?

Tavis wasn't going to allow himself to ponder his reasoning. He simply knew he intended to educate himself more and fast.

Surely his sudden interest in communicable diseases had nothing to do with the spunky ball of fire sleeping in the master bedroom upstairs.

Instead of heading to his own room next to hers, he

grabbed his laptop from the kitchen counter, fired it up, and carried it to the sofa. He kicked off his shoes, spun around to prop his feet on the cushions, and propped the laptop on his knees.

One hour. That's how long he would allow himself to research. And then he would catch some zzz's. He wanted to be up before her in the morning, coffee brewing, armed and ready to face the day.

∼

That was not how things went down, however.

Tavis bolted awake with a gasp. It took him a moment of glancing around to remember where he was and what his assignment had been.

The sun was up. His laptop was still open on his torso, and a piece of paper fluttered to the floor next to him when he moved.

Tavis swung around, set the laptop on the coffee table, and snagged the paper.

I went to the campus to get the lay of the land. Be back in a while.

C

"Fuck." Tavis jumped to his feet, though there was no reason to be in any kind of hurry. He would never find her. He headed for the front window first and looked out. At least she hadn't taken his SUV. Which then begged the question—how had she gotten to the campus?

He scowled, furious with himself as he took the stairs two at a time to the second floor. After a quick shower in the hall bathroom, he headed into the second bedroom to get dressed. Ten minutes later, he was back downstairs, making coffee.

He paced while the coffee brewed. He'd be toast if anything happened to her on the first goddamn day he was supposed to be watching her. Forcing himself to calm down, he grabbed the loaf of bread and popped two slices into the toaster.

A quick glance at his phone told him it was only eight. She'd left extremely early for a woman who'd been so exhausted when she dropped into bed after midnight. Probably just to push his buttons.

And she definitely had pushed his buttons. He was so pissed off with both himself and her that he couldn't even taste the toast as he ate it. He even slathered it with peanut butter and still couldn't swallow properly.

Should he call Ajax or Ryker? Probably. But then three people would be worried instead of one. He knew he wouldn't be in trouble with anyone. It wasn't his fault he'd been assigned to a runner. How was he supposed to know she was this damn careless?

After he finished his coffee, he forced himself to sit at the table with his laptop and continue researching her expertise just to keep his mind occupied. He found more than just information about epidemiology. He found articles Colette herself had written for Johns Hopkins. He read several of them.

There were pictures too. Staged pics to accompany her bio and action shots of her working in a lab. Often she looked very serious with a furrowed brow—especially while working. Some of them showed a softer side of her, smiling even.

She was very pretty. Not the least bit ostentatious. She didn't wear layers of makeup or have fancy haircuts or manicures in any of the pictures. She didn't need any of that shit. She had a natural beauty that shone on its own.

When he switched to her social media, he learned that she didn't post often. Many pictures of her were posted by someone else. A few featured evenings with friends. In those she looked carefree and happy.

Others were of political events, charity auctions, and state dinners. She looked uncomfortable in most of those, her expression strained, her body tense. Colette Loughlin didn't like the political life. She was a scientist. Unpretentious.

Last night he hadn't gotten a good look at her. It had been dark. She'd been angry, tired, frustrated, and about ten other emotions. Perhaps even hungover. Her hair had been in a long braid down her back. Jeans. T-shirt. Tennis shoes. Traveling clothes.

Now, he wondered what her hair would look like when it was down. From the pictures, he could tell it was thick and wavy. She didn't keep some elaborate style that would require multiple trips to the hairdresser. Simple. Easy. Elegant without all the fanfare.

Suddenly the front door opened and Tavis jumped to his feet. His ire rose to the surface immediately. "What the fuck, Colette?"

She shut the door and met his gaze, smirking. Head held high without a single bit of chagrin, she strode toward the kitchen area. "Good morning to you too, Tavis." She grabbed an apple from a bowl on the counter. A bowl of fruit he'd set out.

She took a huge bite and chewed, leaning a hip against the counter.

"We need to talk. Obviously you don't understand the scope of my job." He set his hands on his hips and glared at her.

She shrugged. "Oh, trust me. I understand perfectly. My father thinks I'm twelve and need constant supervision. He's wrong, but he won't listen to me. Believe me, you aren't the first buff guy he's sent to try to control me. And you won't be the last. You're just one in a long line of professional bodyguards hired to make sure nothing imaginary happens to me."

Tavis flinched. She was extremely bitter. Did she have a right to be? He wasn't sure yet, but he intended to find out. "Do you though? Need constant supervision? Because so far it would seem he's right."

She rolled those deep brown eyes and took another bite of her apple. "I'm twenty-seven. I have a master's degree. I've written over a dozen published pieces for several medical journals. I speak four languages fluently. I do not need a keeper."

She shook her apple at him and continued. "Ah, but you already know all that. You sat up late researching me while I slept."

He groaned inwardly at having been caught with his computer in his lap, probably open to an article about her or her research. "How were you so chipper and awake so early in the morning? When you dropped into bed, I thought you might sleep through this entire day."

She chuckled. "I don't need much sleep."

"You were also hungover, weren't you?"

She dropped the apple core in the trash can, set her hands on her hips, and cocked her head at him defiantly. "So now it's a crime to go out drinking with friends? You do realize other grown adults in their late twenties also go out at night, they just don't get followed by the paparazzi and end up on the front page of every fucking tabloid in town."

She had a point. He narrowed his gaze in this odd

standoff. "Look, I don't know you. Well, that's not true. I know everything the tabloids, your social media, and your university have to say, but I don't know enough to judge you. I find it hard to believe you're the sort of person who regularly parties hard and needs a keeper. It doesn't fit with the rest of your bio. Which means I have to believe either your parents don't trust you for some reason, or they refuse to let you grow up, or—and this is the part that worries me—there is an actual threat to your life that has landed me here as your protection."

At least she flinched. "There is no fucking threat. My father is overprotective. He imagines threats. He makes them up. He has for my entire life. In fact, he's gotten worse in the last few years. And you're right about me regularly partying. I don't. How could I even if I wanted to? Someone would follow me and report back to my father."

Tavis took a deep breath. "I think we got off on the wrong foot. How about we start over."

"Nope. We didn't get off on the wrong foot. We started right where I wanted to start. Me making sure you understand that I don't need or want you following me around. I believe I even offered to pay you to stop and give it up."

"Well, that's not an option, princess, so you're going to need to get over yourself. I was hired to keep you safe, and I intend to do just that. Which means if you ever pull a stunt like you did this morning again, I'll assume you have no respect whatsoever for me or my job and take action to ensure we're super clear."

"What are you going to do? Handcuff me to my bed at night?"

"Is that something you enjoy?" He lifted both brows, challenging her.

She flinched. "Of course not. Don't be ridiculous."

He shrugged. "It was your idea. It hadn't even occurred to me. I've never been assigned to be someone's babysitter before. This is new to me. You'll have to let me know what your previous keepers did to ensure you didn't step out of line. I'll take a page from their handbooks. Hey, maybe I can get references from your father and ask them myself."

She narrowed her gaze. "Don't you dare. And I'm not a fucking baby, Rambo. I don't need a sitter or a keeper."

"It would appear you do. If that's the attitude you intend to carry around. This isn't Pennsylvania, princess—"

"*Stop* calling me that," she shouted.

"I like how it gets a rise out of you. Anyway, as I was saying, this is a third-world country we're in. You shouldn't go off half-cocked by yourself under any circumstances, even if no one knew who you were. You don't know enough about this area to take off in the early hours of the morning alone."

"Don't be so dramatic."

"I'm not. I'm being realistic. And you're proving to me that you do indeed need a keeper. So, from now on, don't fucking go anywhere without me, understood? If you do it again, you won't get to have your own bedroom anymore, because trust me, *princess*, I will not hesitate to use the handcuffs you've suggested. And then I'll sleep in the same room just in case you're also Houdini."

"You wouldn't dare."

"Try me." Boy, did she make his blood pump. On top of that, it was hard to keep a straight face. This conversation —if one could even call it a conversation—had deteriorated to the point that it was almost comical. He was afraid she might haul off and slap him if he laughed out loud though.

Damn, she was feisty. And she was under his skin. Not just in a bad way. She was sexy when she got all flustered, especially when he threw her off balance. It was fun.

Suddenly this job didn't seem as bad as he'd been thinking earlier while she'd been AWOL. This banter might actually be fun. She was cute when she got all hot and bothered, making him wonder what she might look like if she were hot and bothered in a different way.

The way she'd reacted to the handcuffs left him curious to know if she'd truly been horrified or if she had a kinky side. And if she had a kinky side, had she ever acted on it or was it just in her imagination and dreams?

He shook those inappropriate thoughts aside. He was here to protect her, not sleep with her.

"Are we done here, *Dad?*" she asked.

Her tone and choice of words made his breath hitch. "How old are you again?"

She groaned and stomped past him, heading for the stairs.

He watched her as she jogged up them. "By the way, princess, I checked the windows up there. They all have permanent bars on them, so don't get any ideas about climbing onto a tree limb and shimmying to freedom."

She growled as she reached the top and then slammed the door to her bedroom.

Oh, yeah. This was going to be fun.

CHAPTER 4

Colette spent most of the rest of the day avoiding Tavis entirely. She stayed in her room, only coming out to get food and returning where she worked on her laptop on her bed.

She didn't need to report to any classes for another few days. She intended to use that time to acclimate herself to the time zone, learn more about Kampala and Uganda, and explore the city a bit.

That last plan was going to be challenging since she didn't relish the idea of wandering around with a freaking bodyguard, but she'd done it for most of her life, so she would endure it now too.

At least he wasn't hard on the eyes. The guy was ripped. Extremely good looking. Nothing like the guys she was usually attracted to. Well, maybe that wasn't true. She often did a double take when she saw buff men like Tavis. She didn't date them because her father would be horrified.

Hell, maybe she should start dating people like Tavis just to infuriate her father. Or, perhaps the only reason why she found him attractive was *because* she knew it would infuriate her father. Hard to say.

Colette preferred to dedicate most of her time to her studies. She'd done that for years. Started in early high school. More than a decade ago. About the time her parents began to foist eligible men on her.

They'd gone round and round when she was about sixteen. Them wanting to choose who she dated, her wanting to pick her own boyfriends. In the end, she'd decided it wasn't worth the hassle and told her parents she wasn't interested in dating at all. She cared more about her studies.

Even though her love of science started as a means to avoid her parents, she'd developed a strong interest in infectious diseases. None of that was untrue. She would dedicate her life to helping save lives.

As for dating, she'd relented on many occasions to appease her parents, attending functions with whomever they thought was appropriate. Nine times out of ten, she found the men to be incredibly boring, narcissistic, or arrogant. She could smell it on them in the first few minutes, and then would make it clear this was a one-time deal. Keep their hands to themselves.

Oddly, few men were offended by her sharp tongue or the fact that she held them at arm's length. They saw her as a challenge. What they probably saw more than anything were dollar signs and connections.

It was amazing what men would put up with because they thought it would help their own career ambitions. Somehow, they would ignore her overt attempts to shut down their advances and pursue her anyway.

So, yeah, it was men like Tavis who caught her eye. Was it in defiance or because she actually found them attractive?

She chuckled quietly as she recalled finding him on the couch sound asleep, his computer open to an article on epidemiology. It was sweet in a way. She doubted any previous bodyguard had taken a single moment to pronounce or spell her chosen profession, let alone google it.

She'd even hesitated for a moment, feeling bad about skipping out on him, knowing he would be furious when he awoke to find her gone. It was kind of cruel. After all, he was only doing his job and she tended to spend most of her time ensuring that her protection was miserable while keeping tabs on her.

She had a pattern. She always slipped past every new bodyguard and took off within the first twenty-four hours. It was her way of letting them know she hated having protection following her around and had no intention of making it easy on them.

Tavis had said something that caught her attention though. Something about her being the first person he'd been assigned as a bodyguard. That was odd. What did he mean? Wasn't guarding people his entire profession?

She hadn't asked yet, but she would because now she was curious. Didn't he work for some sort of protection agency?

The scent of food caused her to unfold herself from where she sat cross-legged on the bed, set her laptop aside, and head downstairs.

"Hey." Tavis smiled at her when she approached tentatively. Why was he smiling? Wasn't he furious with her? She would be if she were him. "Hungry?" he asked.

"Starving. That smells good. What are you making?"

"Spaghetti. The sauce is my mom's recipe. I loved it growing up, so I make it pretty often. A huge batch. We can keep it in the freezer in smaller containers and then just boil pasta when we want some." He glanced at her again. "Do you like red sauce?"

"Adore it. Thank you." She leaned a hip against the counter. "So you cook in addition to your bodyguard services? My father has never hired me a man who could cook too."

Tavis chuckled, which made her heart rate pick up. He was a nice guy. Dammit. She should be kind in return. *It's not his fault your father is overprotective*, she reminded herself.

"It wasn't a job requirement as far as I know, but we've got to eat, and I didn't have anything else to do at the moment, so I cooked." He reached overhead and pulled down two plates, handing them to her. "It's almost ready."

She headed toward the table. Damn. The man had made a salad and bread too. The scent in the air was garlic. Enticing. Her stomach grumbled. She'd eaten very little today, snacks mostly.

"I picked up a few bottles of wine and some beer when I was shopping. I wasn't sure what you might like or even if you were usually a drinker."

She winced as he set the steaming pot of sauce on the table. "Normally, yes. I like a glass of wine with dinner. But I don't think I've fully recovered from my night of defiance yet," she informed him.

He chuckled again. "Is that what it was? A night of defiance?"

"Yes. I was pissed. I went out. I did some things. Not super proud of it."

"Did you feel better afterward?" he asked as he sat across from her.

"Not a bit. I felt hung over. Dehydrated. Headache you would not believe. It was stupid." It was beyond stupid. He didn't even know the half of it.

"Okay. So we save the wine for another time." He pointed at the food. "Go ahead. Dig in. I had no idea if there was anything you don't eat. Allergies? Food you hate? Please tell me you aren't vegan or something."

"Nope. I eat most things. No allergies. Definitely meat." She reached across and set her hand on his, shocking even herself. "And thank you. I mean it."

He shrugged. "I had to eat too."

"Not just for the food but for not lecturing me again. I know I can be a pain in the ass. I'm sorry for being a bratty bitch. Can we start over?"

"Of course." He gave her an odd smile. Or maybe it was a smirk. "But I'm still keeping the handcuffs nearby just in case you're lying to me right now."

She laughed. "I promise not to sneak out in the night."

"What about the day?" He lifted a brow.

She shook her head. "Not then either. Swear."

"Good. I know you hate having protection. You've made that clear. But you're stuck with me, so maybe we can declare a truce of some sort."

"One where you stay here all day and let me go to school without a shadow?" She grinned to make sure it was obvious she knew that wasn't going to happen.

"Hardly. Nice try. But I can attempt to stay out of your way and not hover so you can do your thing. If you give me the lay of the land for the places you'll be, I'll figure out where I can wait unobtrusively for you while still making sure you're safe."

"You do realize no one gives a single fuck about me, right? It's all in my dad's head."

He shrugged. "Maybe. Maybe not. Doesn't matter. I was hired to protect you, and that's what I'm going to do."

She took a bite of spaghetti and moaned around the flavor. "My God, that's good."

"Glad you like it."

"I could get used to this."

He laughed. "Me cooking? Hate to ruin my image, but my repertoire isn't very huge."

"Darn." She took another bite, wiped her lips, and met his gaze again. "I'm curious. You mentioned earlier that you don't usually do this sort of job. How did you end up as my protection detail if you aren't normally a bodyguard?"

"I work for the Holt Agency. Normally we're hired to find missing people, rescue people, things like that. Not protect people who haven't been kidnapped yet." He leaned forward. "And I was hoping *you* could tell *me* why I was hired? There must be two dozen agencies that provide protection. Why did your father call mine?"

She winced. Yeah, she'd stepped right into this mess. "Uh, probably because no one will take my father's calls anymore."

He chuckled. "Figured that was the case. You've burned through a lot of bodyguards, huh?"

She sighed. "Yes. Can't lie. No offense. I don't like being followed. I don't like how people look at me differently when I have some bulky bouncer following me around. I don't like to stand out. I just want to be a regular person."

"I get that."

"It's hard to know if anyone legitimately likes me. I don't mean to sound like I'm in middle school, but you have no idea how many grown women will befriend me just to flirt with my sexy bodyguard."

"So, I'm sexy?"

She rolled her eyes but couldn't keep from chuckling. "Don't let it go to your head." She pointed her fork at his biceps where a tattoo was visible. "Were you in the Navy?"

"Yes. SEALs actually." He lifted a brow.

She whistled. "Ohhh. So you're not some dumb bouncer guy."

"Nope. But I can pretend to be if you'd like."

She laughed. Out loud. "God, no. Please don't. The change will be refreshing."

He set his elbows on the table. "I get why you'd like people to just see you as yourself, so why don't we go over to the university tomorrow. You can show me around. If I know what your schedule is going to look like, I can figure something out that keeps me sort of hidden at first."

She swallowed. "You'd do that?"

"Of course."

She stared at him, taking deep breaths. His expression was intense. Serious. He wasn't an asshole. He was a good guy who'd been saddled with her. He didn't want this either.

She shifted her weight when she realized her heart was beating faster. She squeezed her thighs together under the table. Lordy, she was aroused. She didn't even know how to process that detail. It was foreign to her. Not many men had ever elicited such a reaction from her, and certainly none of her assigned security detail.

She licked her lips. "Thank you," she murmured.

"Any time." He pointed at her dinner. "Eat before it gets cold. Then you can show me your schedule. Tomorrow we can do a walk-through."

They ate in silence until they were finished and then she asked him more questions as they cleaned the kitchen. "How long were you in the Navy?"

"Seventeen years."

"Why did you get out?"

"Long story. For another time. But I've been with the Holt Agency about a year. Started it up with the rest of my team after we were medically discharged."

"Oh. So this is new to you."

"Yes. I mean, I've been on several missions so far. My last was here in Uganda. I was at the airport about to leave the country when my boss called and dumped you in my lap." He gave her a goofy grin.

She bumped his hip with hers, though it ended up being more like his thigh since he was so much taller than her. "I deserve that."

"You do," he agreed. "Am I going to need the handcuffs?"

She gave him a coy look and shrugged before she could stop herself. "We'll see."

His brows shot up high on his forehead.

Her face heated to a hundred degrees. "Please tell me I did not just say that out loud."

When he laughed this time, something shifted inside her. She really liked that sound. And his playfulness. And how understanding he was being. But she shouldn't be hitting on him.

He didn't mention it again, and when they were finished, she retrieved her laptop and sat down at the table with him to go over her schedule.

"How did you become interested in epidemiology?" he asked as she shut the laptop.

She sighed. "It's kinda lame."

"Okay. I can listen to lame stories. Will I need coffee to stay awake?"

She laughed. How did he keep making her laugh? "Probably. Or maybe just throw a pity party for me when I'm done."

"I didn't get any balloons at the store, but I could probably make party hats out of paper if you want."

She laughed again and pushed from the table. "Let's move to the couch."

He followed her and settled on one end while she sat on the other. She angled herself sideways, leaned her back against the arm of the couch, and drew her legs up under her. "So, my parents are fixated on setting me up with men, a long string of whoever they think is appropriate."

"For such a debutante as yourself of course," he teased.

"Exactly." She rolled her eyes. "I was born into the wrong family. There was a mix-up of some sort with the stork."

His entire chest shook when he chuckled this time.

"I've never fit the mold. I hate being in the spotlight. I hate politics. I hate rich people. I hate money to be honest. All it does is cause problems."

"So, not only do you not want your new coworkers at the university to know you have a bodyguard, but you don't want them to think you're rich either."

"Right." She nodded. "They'll find out if they haven't already, but I like to buy time. It helps me know who likes me for myself first."

"Makes sense. Go on. Get back to the epidemiology choice."

She drew in a breath, staring at him for a few moments. He was sincere. He wanted to know. He hadn't looked away or picked up his phone to check messages. He hadn't turned on the television. He wanted to hear what she had to say. Had anyone ever been this legitimately respectful to her?

"Anyway, by the time I was in high school, my mother in particular started trying to fix me up with her friends' sons. It was embarrassing and humiliating. And I can't tell you how stuffy those rich white boys are." She cringed. "Sorry. That sounds crass."

He shrugged. "It's okay. I'm not offended."

"I didn't want to date any of them. Or anyone else

really. So, I buried myself in my schoolwork to keep my parents from bothering me. I realized I loved science and it snowballed from there. At some point in college, I narrowed my emphasis to epidemiology and later refined that to specifically malaria and AIDS."

"Damn. You must be incredibly smart. I mean I know you are. I read some of your published articles. I'm impressed."

She cringed. "You read that stuff?"

"Most of it. It was a bit over my head. I'm just a dumb bouncer, ya know," he teased.

"Sorry. I shouldn't have stereotyped you. You're not dumb. Nor are you apparently a bouncer. Though you could be with those biceps. How many hours a day do you work out?"

"Depends." There was a twinkle in his eyes that made her smile, wondering what he would say next. "If I can trust you not to run, I'll jog in the mornings and then do some weight training."

"I guess you could always cuff me to the bed before you leave." Her face flushed again. Where was she getting these flirty comeback lines?

"If that's what you want, I'll be happy to." He winked. "Watch what you dish out, princess."

She rolled her head back and groaned. "Could we stop with the princess? Pick another nickname for me. Anything else."

"I'll have to think about that," he mused.

CHAPTER 5

Colette was beyond impressed with Tavis's willingness to work with her. Every previous man her father had employed had been inflexible and demanding. Perhaps it helped that Tavis hadn't spoken to her father directly. His agency had been hired to do a job. He'd simply been the man assigned.

He was patient and thorough, taking note of where each of her classes would be located, the days and times, and then scouring the area to figure out where he could wait unobtrusively so that no one noticed him.

"You planning to dress like a student and carry a backpack?" she teased when he pointed to a park bench outside one of her classes.

He looked down at her. "Why not? It'll work."

"Oh." That was new too then. "So, no black slacks, dark glasses, earpieces, ties?"

"Don't own any of those things. Told you I'm not a bodyguard." He smirked. "Do you need me to have a uniform?"

"God, no. I'm relieved. If you're serious, I might actually

pull this off. Maybe no one will notice you." She glanced at him as they returned to the car and chuckled. "Never mind. No chance of that. Everyone will notice you. Maybe they won't realize you're with me."

He opened the car door and waited for her to climb inside before shutting it and rounding the hood. When he was settled in his seat, he continued. "I can't make promises, Colette. I won't jeopardize your safety at any point. I'll do my best to remain anonymous for as long as possible, but not if I feel like it's not safe. I don't like rooms with two entrances, for example. When I can't see you with my eyes, I need to know at the very least what exit you'll be coming from."

"If you could just buy me a few days. Or a week. That would be great. Let me establish relationships before people notice you," she pleaded.

He glanced at her when he came to a stop. "Just so we're clear, you get one shot at proving to me that you're working with me and not against me. If you're setting this all up as an elaborate stunt to escape me, you'll find yourself so glued to my side for the next six months you'll rue the day you crossed me. Understood?"

She sighed. "I get that you don't trust me. Can't blame you. But I promise I won't flee."

He pulled up to the condo and she scrambled down from her seat before he had a chance to help her out. He waited for her, looking around as he did so, and then ushered her in front of him as they headed for the door.

Every bodyguard she'd ever had had done similar things. Somehow with Tavis, it felt different. Like he was a gentleman instead of doing a job. She would bet, based on what he'd said about his mother, he'd been raised to treat women a certain way that came naturally to him and wasn't just a job.

"Keep in mind," he said as they entered, "the university is informed about me. I have paperwork on me at all times indicating who I am and what my assignment is. I can't have someone chasing me off the campus because I seem suspicious. I'm not buying you a semester of anonymity. Just a few days."

"Got it."

"I don't need to come inside rooms with you, Colette, but I'd feel much better if I were stationed outside the door, not the building." He lifted a brow.

"Okay. Okay. A few days, please."

"Yep." He smiled. "And don't make me bring out those handcuffs."

Ah, so playful Tavis is back. "Just out of curiosity, do you actually have handcuffs?"

"Of course." He didn't flinch.

She did. And then she glanced up and down his frame. He was wearing a long-sleeved untucked shirt over jeans. He had on comfortable boots and had carried a backpack slung over his shoulder all morning.

"I'm armed, Colette. At all times. I'm a former SEAL. I have skills that far exceed any of your previous bodyguards and the equipment to go with it." He stepped closer, making her breath hitch. "And, just for the record, I'm not remotely convinced you're in no danger."

She drew in a breath. "What makes you say that?"

He shrugged. "Intuition. Has anyone ever bothered you before?"

She dropped her shoulders. "No one worth mentioning."

He lifted a brow. "Everyone who has even glanced at you sideways is worth mentioning, Colette." He pointed at the couch. "Sit. Tell me everything that's ever been even remotely suspicious. Don't leave out a single detail."

She sighed as she dropped onto the couch. "It's not that interesting, Tavis. I'm not kidding. Mostly guys in bars who recognize me and hit on me, or sometimes guys in bars who *don't* recognize me and *still* hit on me."

"You said you don't go to many bars," he pointed out as he dropped onto the other end of the sofa and angled himself to face her.

"I don't, but you wanted every sordid detail."

"When was the last time a guy bothered you in a bar?"

She laughed. "Two nights ago before I left town?"

He frowned. "Was anyone with you besides your posse?"

"Nope. I snuck out like an underage grounded teenager. It's what I do when I'm displeased with my father."

"Why?" He looked genuinely confused, brow furrowed and all. "You're twenty-seven. By all counts brilliant, overly educated, good head on your shoulders. Why such defiance?"

"I've told you. I hate being followed all the time. This thing…" She waved a hand between them to indicate both of them. "You seem like a nice enough guy. So far, I'm relieved to have someone in my space I can at least carry on a conversation with and not feel like I'm tiptoeing around. You have no idea how frustrating it is to have some giant, silent, overbearing man standing in my damn space all the time, watching me. Hovering. I can't even be myself, be comfortable in my own space." She shuddered.

"Has other protection been paid to stay *inside* your apartment before?"

"No." She shook her head. "Never. This is a first."

"Well, this is a third-world country. There's more danger than what you're used to in the States."

"I did enough research to know this is a relatively safe

place. There are more dangerous spots in North America than here."

"True, on the whole, but if there is any kind of ongoing threat to your life, this is the perfect place for someone to try to act on it. The police can be bought for a small fee here."

She sighed.

Tavis watched her closely. "Have you had any trouble with any of your bodyguards?"

"What kind of trouble?" she asked, glancing at her lap and then picking imaginary lint from her jeans. Tavis was so intrusive.

"Whatever trouble has made you glance away to avoid eye contact." He leaned forward. "Colette." His voice was firm. Demanding.

She glanced up. "Not a big deal. Some of them have made me uncomfortable at times. Wandering eyes and shit."

"Leering at you when they were supposed to be guarding you?"

She shrugged. "Sometimes." She shoved off the couch and headed for the kitchen area to grab a water and break up this line of questioning.

When she spun back around from the fridge, she nearly jumped out of her skin. A gasp escaped her lips. Tavis was right behind her, hands on his hips. He reached out quickly to steady her when she swayed.

"Sorry. Didn't mean to scare you. Elaborate. Right now."

"I don't feel like it, okay? It's embarrassing."

He shook his head. "Nope. Not okay. Spill. Every detail of anything that's ever been even remotely unprofessional with a bodyguard. Don't leave out a single thing."

She took a sip of water and set it on the island. "Most

things were my fault. In my first few years of college, I used to flirt with them rather mercilessly. I probably looked like a complete fool. I have no skills at flirting. I was antagonizing them to infuriate my parents more than anything."

He chuckled. At least he wasn't quite as serious and stern. "I'm struggling to picture this, but no matter how much you may have flirted with any of them, they shouldn't have responded. They were there to do a job. Period."

She scrunched up her face. "I probably took things a bit too far a few times. Traipsing around in my towel or half dressed."

He lifted a brow. "Did any of them approach you inappropriately?"

"No." She rolled her eyes dramatically. "Told you, I'm not good at flirting." She brushed past Tavis, hoping this line of questioning was over.

He reached out and grabbed her biceps to stop her.

Her breath hitched at the contact. He was so close and smelled so good, and she liked how it felt to have his fingers around her arm. She didn't lift her gaze. Embarrassed mostly.

How ironic that she was telling him all about her flirting antics from the past while she had the overwhelming urge to literally throw herself at this man. She may have flaunted herself in front of others, but that had been a game. This time it was real. She liked Tavis. Or at least she was physically attracted to him in a way she'd never really experienced before.

He slowly released her. His voice was lower when he spoke. "You're avoiding my questions entirely and you know it. I don't care about what you did at eighteen to get your security detail to notice you. I want to know what any of them ever did to get *you* to notice *them*."

"Doesn't matter because it was unsuccessful." She shrugged him off, still not looking up, beyond aware of his proximity, especially when he stepped closer.

"Colette..." He reached out with a finger and lifted her chin. His eyes were narrowed with concern.

"Fine." She rolled her eyes. "A few years ago, one of them made a pass at me. Several passes actually. I told him I wasn't interested and tried to ignore him. I didn't want to have to tell my father what was happening because I didn't think he would believe me after the shit I had pulled in my late teens."

"What happened then?"

"I decided to lose him. Permanently. I snuck away while he was in the shower and went to some friends' apartment and hid out for two weeks."

"Shit. Did you tell your parents where you were?"

"I messaged them that I was safe and to call off their dog or I wouldn't come back out of hiding. It worked. They fired him for losing me, which was exactly what I wanted."

"And that was it? He left and never came back? You've never seen him again?"

"Nope. Done and gone. Don't even care if the door hit him in the ass on his way out or not." She angled around Tavis and headed for the stairs, needing space. He made her tongue tied.

"Colette... I'm not done."

She turned on the first step and faced him. "Could we table this?"

"No." He followed her.

She continued up the stairs. Maybe he wouldn't press further if she fled.

"Do you always walk away from people when they're talking to you?" he asked, hot on her heels. Maybe he would follow her.

"Actually, yes," she tossed over her shoulder. "When it's a topic I don't want to discuss." She could feel his breath on her neck. He was one step behind her.

"Can you tell me why?" He followed her into her bedroom.

She spun around and faced him. "Already told you. It's embarrassing."

He inhaled slowly and then spoke in a level voice. "I have two more issues, and then I'll leave you alone. Tell me what happened the night before you flew here."

Colette shook her head. "Not a chance in hell. Everything you need to know was probably flashed all over social media."

"Were there any men I need to be worried about from that night?"

"Nope," she lied. "Just me and my friends out drinking too much and dancing. Like regular humans are wont to do."

He stared at her a minute, not buying her story. "Okay, fine. Keep your secrets. For now. You don't lie well though. One other thing—"

She put out a hand. "No. No more things. I don't want to discuss my stupid love life with you." She set her palm on his chest in attempt to push him out of the room.

He didn't budge, but he did set his hand on top of hers.

She shoved her entire body into him, hip first, trying to get him to back up. "Tavis, please." Her heart was racing. Her body was shaking. She'd gone from sort of hot for him to full-on flammable.

Everything about him crawled under her skin like no man ever had in her life. She'd never been so attracted to anyone in all her twenty-seven years. She'd spent less than two days with him and for most of that time she'd had wet panties and stiff nipples.

He was going to see through her any minute, and then she'd be far more mortified than she already was.

Why was she touching him? It was only making things worse. And she was acting like a lunatic in her desperation to put some distance between them.

Every time he spoke, his words sent shivers up her spine. His tone or something. She couldn't put her finger on it. And dammit, but he seemed to care. As if he really wanted to get to the bottom of her imaginary threat. Her other bodyguards just did their jobs. They didn't speak more than necessary. They didn't ask questions. They just guarded her because her father paid them to.

Tavis was pushy and insistent. Inquisitive. In her face. He'd said he wasn't a bodyguard at all. No wonder. He clearly didn't know the rules or what his job was or that he should just watch her and leave her alone.

She gave another shove. He didn't budge an inch, but his fingers wrapped around hers against his chest and squeezed. "Talk to me," he stated calmly.

"No. Get out." She said the words, but there was no force behind them, and she was glad there weren't cameras in the room because a replay of this would be humiliating.

His free hand came to the back of her head and he pulled her flush against him, pressing her face into his chest next to their combined hands.

She breathed heavily, her entire body shooting through the roof with arousal. The way he cupped the back of her head. The way he stroked her fingers in his fist. The way he started whispering kind words to her.

"Shhh. You're okay. Take a deep breath."

She inhaled long and slow, furious for following his orders.

"There you go. Let it out."

When she did so, he continued. "Now, why are you trying to push me away?"

She tipped her head back and met his gaze. "Why are you trying to pry so much information out of me?"

"Because I want you to be safe."

"Why not just follow me around like everyone else and not worry about the past?"

"Because I care about more than my paycheck. Because you deserve a life that doesn't make you feel like you're suffocating."

She drew in another breath. "Okay, fine. What's your last concern?" The fastest way to get him out of her room was obviously to answer his damn question. And she desperately needed him to leave her room before he realized how affected she was by him. How humiliating.

His brows drew together and he threaded his fingers in her hair. "It hasn't slipped my attention that while my hackles are raised about any former bodyguard you've had that may have behaved inappropriately toward you, I've broken every rule in my own playbook, including currently holding you in my arms."

She swallowed hard. "Well, it turns out I kinda like it. And it's also scary. And I'm not used to feeling like this." She was trembling in his grip. *Why the hell did I just tell him all that? Jesus.* This was why she needed him gone.

"Okay. I'm going to apologize and back off and leave you be, but I want you to do something for me."

She nodded. At the moment she was putty in his hands, an odd feeling that made her nervous.

"Please think back. If you can recall anyone from any time who might have a reason to be disgruntled with you, no matter how farfetched it might seem, please tell me so I can look into it."

"Okay." She frowned. "I still don't understand why you think there's any threat. Why can't you just accept that my father is overprotective?"

He shrugged. "Humor me."

CHAPTER 6

"Ryker. How's it going?" Tavis asked him when he placed his late-night call after Colette went to bed.

"Going well here. How about there? I heard your latest assignment might be a handful."

Tavis chuckled. "Yeah, I think I nipped that in the bud. Hopefully. Can you do me a favor and have someone look into Colette's past bodyguards?"

Ryker whistled. "That's quite a list."

"Yeah, I know. Maybe gloss over most of them. See where they are and what they're doing. I'm most interested in the one who hit on her a few years back and got fired."

"Will do. I'm sure I can get a list from someone in her father's office."

"That's what I'm hoping."

"Anything else?"

Tavis glanced at the stairs. He was sitting in the living room. Colette hadn't opened the door since she'd offered an awkward goodnight a few hours ago, but he didn't want her to hear him. "Can you dig a little deeper into what transpired the night before she flew here?"

"Sure thing. I know she slipped out undetected, but there were pictures and I can probably pinpoint destinations and times from credit card reports."

Tavis ran his hand over his head. He hated going behind her back and digging around in her private life, but he also thought she was holding back. Something happened that night. He'd bet money on it. "Thanks."

"Okay, you just keep doing that cushy job in Kampala. We'll do all the hard work over here," Ryker joked.

Tavis rolled his eyes even though no one could see him. "Wanna trade? Six months here following around a grad student versus holding down the fort in Indiana with Xena by your side?" he shot back, teasingly.

"Nope. I'm good. I'll call you when I have anything interesting."

"Later." Tavis ended the call, rubbed his eyes, and shoved to standing. He needed sleep.

He needed to put what happened earlier out of his head. He never should have touched Colette in the first place. He'd been in the middle of mentally reprimanding every previous bodyguard who'd had the balls to even glance at her while he'd reached out and grabbed her arm.

They'd brushed against each other in the kitchen a few times prior, but that was the first time he'd blatantly wrapped his fingers around her warm skin. He had no idea why he'd done it. He shouldn't have.

Nor should he have grabbed her hand when she shoved at his chest. And he definitely shouldn't have cupped the back of her head, held her against him, and threaded his fingers in her soft hair.

He wasn't sure why or how he'd had the balls to point all of that out, but he'd nearly choked when she'd admitted that she'd liked his touch.

Shit.

What a mess. This was a job, not someone he could fuck on the side. He was supposed to protect her for the next six months. Not sleep with her.

From the moment he'd gripped her hand and felt her thick hair running between his fingers, he'd been hard. How he'd managed to cook dinner alongside her and make small talk was a miracle.

He'd left her in her room for a few hours, but when she'd emerged to cook with him, she'd pretended nothing had happened between them. That was fine. For now. Not forever, but for a while.

He headed to bed, pausing at the top of the stairs to stare at her closed door. What did she really wear to bed? She'd insinuated the first night that she'd intended to strip down to her panties and climb between the sheets.

Lord knows it had been difficult for him to slowly wander from corner to corner of her bed lowering the mosquito netting after that declaration. At that point, he'd only known her for about an hour, and she'd been nothing but combative with him, but somehow, he'd already been drawn to her.

He liked that she was feisty and determined. Not to mention gorgeous even after traveling for nearly thirty hours.

He smiled as he stared at her door and then swiped his hand down his face to wipe away the inappropriate grin. Turning toward his own room, he took a deep breath. "Let it go," he muttered. "Don't even think about starting something with her."

∼

The next week flew by as Tavis settled into his odd assignment. Neither of them mentioned a word about their exchange the night he'd held her in his arms. Hopefully she'd recognized the same as him that nothing could happen between them because if she ever blinked at him again with that same expression of desire, he wasn't sure how strong he could be.

True to her word, she didn't evade him again. And in exchange, true to *his* word, he kept himself out of sight so that no one realized she had a protection detail following her around.

Tavis thought he did a pretty good job pretending to be a student. He carried around a backpack, dressed casually, and spent a lot of time on his laptop when she was in class. It worked out perfectly. He was able to dig deeper into each of her previous bodyguards, helping the main office figure out where every one of them was and what they were doing now.

He also scoured the internet behind her back to find more details about her Houdini act from the night before she'd left. He still suspected that night hadn't gone exactly smoothly. Every time the subject came up, she hedged, changed the subject, and didn't meet his gaze.

Maybe she was embarrassed for drinking too much and partying too hard. No reason to be. There was nothing wrong with having fun with her friends. Hell, he'd be a hypocrite to criticize her for overindulging. Who hadn't done so, especially in their twenties?

All he'd found so far were pics on two of her friends' social media platforms and one single credit card charge. She must have picked up that particular tab while someone else handled the others. Also not suspicious. Each woman would have bought a round.

Tavis was uncomfortable with the fact that no one could track down the location or any details about the particular bodyguard who'd been fired. At least they now knew his name. Steve Lacoste. Where the hell was the man now? He couldn't have simply vanished.

When they returned to the apartment Friday afternoon, Colette was quiet. Too quiet.

"Everything okay?" he asked once they were safely inside, not wanting to pressure her in the car.

"Mmm hmm," she responded without looking at him. "Just tired." She took the stairs two at a time and disappeared into her room.

Tavis didn't like it. The two of them had gradually thawed to each other over the past week. Colette hadn't been combative or tried to evade him a single time. He also didn't think anyone from her department had picked up on the fact that she had security following her around. If they had, she hadn't said a word.

He made dinner alone and then rapped on her door with his knuckles. "Colette? I cooked. You want to come out and eat?"

"Uh, sure. Give me a minute. I'll be down." Her voice was raised enough for him to hear her.

Five minutes later she met him in the kitchen, still not looking at him.

"Talk to me," he encouraged. "Something's obviously bothering you. Is it about me? Did someone figure out you have protection?"

She shook her head. "No. Everything's fine." She stabbed into a vegetable from the stir-fry he'd made and stuffed it into her mouth.

"Everything is clearly not fine." He still hadn't taken a bite. He leaned back in his chair to stare at her.

She finally glanced up at him. "No big deal, okay? Can you just let it go? It's personal."

He held her gaze, uncertain he liked this plan. *Personal?* As in she started her period or something? He definitely didn't need to hear the details about that if it were the case. Nor did he know her well enough to be aware of her mood swings. So, he'd leave it alone for now. "Okay."

When they finished eating, she insisted on cleaning the kitchen and then bolted to shut herself in her room again.

It was a long weekend. Colette had changed. Her mood remained sullen and withdrawn. By Monday, he wanted to shake the information out of her, but refrained. At least she gradually came back into herself throughout the week.

"How about if we go to Sipi Falls this weekend?" he suggested on Wednesday. "I've heard the hiking and waterfalls are amazing."

She actually perked up at that suggestion. "Sounds like fun. Let's do it."

"I'll make reservations. I've heard the Sipi Falls Lodge is beautiful. Glamping, I think you'd call it. Fancy cabins that are rather rustic but gorgeous with amazing views."

She smiled. "Perfect."

Colette's classes ended early on Fridays, so they arrived at the falls before dark.

"My God, this is fantastic," she said as she twisted around to take in the views while he checked in. It didn't take long before a porter showed them to their individual cabin and left them to get settled before dinner.

Colette didn't stop smiling as she looked around, taking in the interior before stepping out onto the patio to enjoy the view of the waterfalls.

Tavis met her out there, hoping this return to her much more enjoyable mood might be permanent. "I hope you don't mind sharing the cabin with me. I don't think it would be safe to leave you alone and get my own. There're two beds at least."

She glanced over at him. "It's fine." Her gaze returned to

the view. "Can you believe this? How do they arrange these cabins so that each of them has a perfect view of the falls?"

"It is spectacular," he said, unable to keep from smiling. He took a moment to absorb the view of the waterfalls, but then settled his gaze on her. She was lighter today. Content. Her face was softer, not so drawn in frustration. Maybe if he arranged more trips like this to see the sights in Uganda, she would relax some. Maybe her work in the lab during the week was simply taxing and stressful.

After a delicious dinner and sampling a few regional beers in the lodge, they went to bed. Tavis did everything he could to keep things from being awkward. They had to share the bathroom, and he wasn't about to budge on getting separate rooms. Luckily, she didn't question him.

"They don't have mosquito nets here," she pointed out. "I guess the altitude is too high for mosquitoes."

"Yes. That's my understanding. There are several tourist locations around Uganda, some higher than others. If you want to do a bit of traveling around the country while you're here, I'll look into a trip to the other side of Uganda we can take during your fall break. Maybe a few days of safari? We could also see gorillas if you want."

"That would be wonderful. Do you mind making arrangements?"

"Not at all." He was more than happy to. After spending almost a month in this country, he'd learned more about the most important tourist attractions. He was certainly being paid handsomely enough to afford several side trips. Might as well enjoy everything Uganda had to offer while protecting his grad student.

The morning started with breakfast set up on picnic tables outside the lodge before Tavis secured walking sticks, bottles of water, and directions. They headed up the path to the top of the waterfalls.

Colette was in far better shape than he'd expected for someone who seemed to spend all of her time buried in a science lab. He let her hike in front of him to set the pace, but she rarely slowed down except to take in the views, and there were a lot of spectacular stops along the way to take pictures.

Spending the day with Colette was no hardship either. She was a pleasure. No, she was more than that. Tavis had to remind himself over and over that this wasn't a date. She wasn't his girlfriend like everyone at the lodge assumed. He was being paid to protect her.

It was hard to remember every time he reached out to take her hand to help her up a slippery slope or steadied her with a hand on her back. It was even harder when she made him lean in close for a selfie at various scenic locations.

He offered to take pictures of her alone with the waterfalls in the background, and sometimes she accepted, but more often than not, she reached out her arm and snapped a shot of the two of them together.

After a late lunch and then a nap, they went with a guide to a sunset hike where they were granted a full panoramic view of the area for miles. By the time they sat down for dinner back at the lodge that night, Tavis knew he was in deep trouble.

He was falling hard for this woman. His attraction was undeniable and growing by the day. Even though he didn't mention it, judging by the flush that frequently covered her cheeks and the way she smiled at him, she felt the same way.

They moved over to sit in front of the fireplace in the lodge after dinner, sipping a glass of wine and staring at the flames. "Tell me about your childhood," he prompted.

Colette glanced at him and then turned back to the fire.

"Wish I could say it was typical, but that would be a lie. As the only child of a prominent lawyer and politician always climbing the ladder of success, I was raised to be the perfect lady." She winced.

"What does the perfect lady look like?"

"Arm candy."

"Yikes." He cringed. It was hard to picture Colette fitting that mold. And based on what she'd told him, she didn't. Not even close.

She shot him a grin. "Remember I told you the stork delivered me to the wrong house."

He chuckled. What he wanted to do was grab her hand. Run his finger over her knuckles. Lift it to his lips and kiss her palm. Instead, he held her gaze.

After several seconds, she looked away and drew in a breath. "Anyway, I went to private schools. Took piano lessons. Horseback riding. Golf."

He curled up his nose. "Golf? You?"

"'Never know when you might need to impress a man with your golf skills,'" she said in a deep voice, apparently imitating her father.

"Do you play now?"

"God, no. It's awful. I hope I never have to touch a golf club again. Do you play?" She shot him a glance.

"Never tried it a single time. Doesn't interest me either."

"What about you?" she asked, changing the subject. "Tell me about your childhood."

"Well, I grew up in Virginia. Also an only child. My parents were older. They have since passed away. They didn't have the funds to afford college for me, so I joined the Navy, mostly because several of my friends enlisted out of high school. But I had high aspirations and worked my ass off to make the SEAL team."

"And you left the SEALs recently. You didn't tell me why," she pointed out.

"Yeah. Long story. I'll give you the cliff notes. I was captured in an attack with most of my team and spent three months in captivity in Ethiopia before being rescued."

She turned to more fully face him, grabbing his arm. "Oh, my God. That's awful."

He shrugged. "We all escaped relatively unscathed, but we formed a deep bond from the experience, were all medically discharged, and started our own company. That's when the Holt Agency came into being. I love my job. Wouldn't change it for the world."

"And that job does not entail protecting seemingly wild debutantes who don't fit the mold."

He reached for her hand that was gripping his wrist, turned his palm over, and threaded their fingers together. Huge step. Crossing every line known to mankind. He couldn't stop himself. "No," he murmured. "But I'm not sorry I'm here."

"Me neither," she whispered in response.

He gave her hand a squeeze and stood. "Come on. Let's get some sleep. Tomorrow we're visiting a coffee plantation before we head back to Kampala."

She rose, not releasing his fingers.

His heart was pounding as he led her back to their cabin, and as soon as they were inside, he dropped her hand to shut and lock the door. When he turned around, he found she hadn't moved an inch. She was right in front of him.

Neither of them had turned on the lights, but there was enough illumination coming through the windows from the moon.

She tentatively set her palms on his chest and tipped her head back.

Tavis set his hands on her waist, his fingers spanning her lower back. He shouldn't do this. The line was blurring further by the second. "Colette…"

"I swear I've never seriously hit on a single bodyguard before," she declared. "There have been a few I flirted with, but only to infuriate my father. I was never serious. I never actually took things farther with them. I never actually felt a connection with any of them before."

He pulled her closer and set his forehead against hers. "You're not making my job easy here, Colette."

"I know," she whispered. "I've been trying to ignore my attraction. I know it's unprofessional and inappropriate and ten other things, but it's still there. All the time. Why can't you be rude or withdrawn or quiet or something?" she joked.

He chuckled. "Because it's mutual. But this is dangerous territory. We should take a step back. If we don't, things will get complicated."

"I know."

That wasn't what he wanted. He wanted to spin her around, press her against the wall, and kiss the sense out of her. He wanted to smooth his hands around to her front, slide them upward, and cup her breasts. He wanted to make her moan. He wanted to reach between her legs and cup her pussy until her knees grew wobbly.

He squeezed his eyes closed and gritted his teeth for a moment.

"You're not going to kiss me, are you?" she asked softly.

"No."

She drew in a breath and turned around.

The last thing he wanted was to hurt her feelings though. It was a fine line. So, he reached out, slid his hands around her waist, and hauled her back against his front. Holding her tight, his arms beneath her breasts, he lowered his lips to her ear. "I want to kiss you more than I want to take my next breath, Colette," he growled. "Do not misunderstand. But I'm not going to. Not tonight. Okay?"

She gasped and nodded slightly. "Yes." Her voice was breathy. Her chest was heaving.

He released her and stepped back, hoping she hadn't noticed how hard his cock was. "Get ready for bed." He rounded to her front, cupped her cheek, and kissed her temple. It was all he would allow himself.

He had little doubt things between them were about to move to a new level, but he didn't want to rush it. They both needed to think hard about what they were doing first.

Tavis was certain her father would lose his shit if he knew that his daughter's bodyguard wanted to get her naked and make her scream his name.

Colette used the bathroom first and slid into her bed while he entered to brush his teeth.

He came to her side and set a hand on her shoulder before heading for his own bed. "You okay?"

"Yes." She grabbed his hand and gave it a squeeze, releasing him just as quickly.

It took a while to fall asleep, but he eventually talked his cock into standing down and let sleep take him under.

CHAPTER 7

Luckily, the tension between them wasn't unmanageable the next day, and they had an amazing time learning about every aspect involved in the process of making coffee from the plant to the mug.

Tavis fired more questions at Colette on the drive back to her apartment, learning more about her with every answer. He'd already known she was brilliant and studious, but apparently that extended way back. She'd been a voracious reader as a child and won a spelling bee in the third grade. She'd also been on the robotics team in middle school and played the violin in high school.

Colette was incredibly well-rounded and had enjoyed every imaginable perk that came with a wealthy upbringing. She'd even giggled as she'd described her ballet and gymnastics days—which apparently hadn't gone so well in her opinion. Tavis wished he could see videos of her as a child in her costumes, twirling around the floor with her apparent two left feet.

It was dark when he pulled up to the apartment, and he immediately knew something was wrong. He grabbed her hand to keep her from opening her car door. "Don't move. Stay here."

Tavis popped the glove compartment and palmed his weapon before exiting the SUV.

"Tavis…" Colette murmured.

He glanced at her.

"Be careful."

He nodded and held the gun close as he approached the front door. It stood ajar, and when he entered the apartment, he groaned. The place was ransacked. "Dammit," he muttered, lifting his gun.

There wasn't a sound coming from anywhere, so he felt confident whoever had broken in had done so earlier, but he moved from room to room downstairs and upstairs to confirm before returning to the car.

"They're gone, aren't they?" Colette asked when he opened her door.

"Yeah." He grabbed their bags from the back of the SUV and followed her inside. "I need to make some calls," he informed her. "Can you see if anything is missing?"

"Yes." She stood rooted for a moment, running her hands through her hair. "Jesus. What a mess. Do you think they were looking for something?"

"I was going to ask you that. Do you have anything here worth stealing?"

"No. Nothing. You saw how I travel. Light. The most valuable things I own are in my head or a cloud. I didn't even leave my computer here."

"Jewelry?" He opened his phone as he asked.

She shook her head. "No." She held out her hands. "I'm pretty minimal. I only brought these few rings and a couple pairs of earrings. Nothing real. No diamonds."

He reached for her hand and gripped it. "Go check around, okay?"

She drew in a ragged breath and nodded. "Jesus," she muttered again as she headed past the kitchen. Pots and pans and plates and every imaginable thing were strewn out all over the room.

Tavis placed his call.

Seconds later, a male voice answered, "Ajax here."

"Hey. It's Tavis. Our apartment got ransacked while we were away for the weekend."

"Fuck," he muttered. "Any clues?"

"No. We just got here, but it looks like they were either looking for something or simply wanted to make a point. I don't like it."

"Stay on her."

Tavis sighed. "Yeah, she's not going to like me hovering closer, but I will be from now on."

"You think you need to move to another location?" Ajax asked.

"Not sure what good it will do. Anyone who wanted could follow us home from her classes."

Tavis could hear the exasperation in Ajax's sigh. "I'll dig into things a bit from here. Did she call her father?"

"No. I doubt she'd willingly do that. I'll do it."

"Okay. Keep me posted."

"Will do." Tavis ended the call and turned around to find Colette stalking toward him, brows furrowed. She snagged his phone out of his hand and set it on the counter. "I assume from your last statement you intend to call my father."

"Yes."

"How about not?" she proposed as she flattened her palms on his chest.

He gripped her biceps and ran his hands up and down. "It's my job, hon. I'm paid to make sure you're safe. When there's a threat, I have to let him know."

"Maybe this was random. Someone hoping to find something valuable and failing."

"Maybe. Maybe not." He lifted a brow.

She slid her hands up around his neck. "You're here. I'm totally safe. He'll insist I come home."

Tavis slid his hands around to her back. He shouldn't be doing this. Yet again, he was too close to her. "If you're trying to soften me up, you will not succeed. I won't keep details from your father. I can't. Don't ask me to. Not even if you bat those pretty eyes at me."

She batted them again, exaggeratingly faster, tipping her head to one side and then rising onto her toes and kissing him.

Her lips were soft and sweet and took him by surprise. He kissed her back, keeping it as light as possible before easing her a few inches away. "Colette…"

"What?"

"Don't you dare use sex as a weapon," he warned.

She dropped her forehead to his chest and leaned in closer.

He didn't release her, keeping her close with his hands splayed on her lower back, letting her think.

Finally, she looked up at him again. "Sorry. That was uncalled for. I know you have to call my father. Can you wait at least an hour until he's out of church? It's Sunday. It will cause him to panic less."

"Yes. I can do that."

"Now, will you kiss me for real? It felt nice."

"Nice?" He smirked.

She rolled her eyes. "Okay, better than nice. I bet we can improve on it."

"Should we though?"

"Yes." The woman was persistent. No way was he going to be able to put her off much longer. He ached for her. It felt like he'd been dating her for months after spending every day together for two weeks. Months was a lot of dates to go on before kissing a woman.

It was too late to turn this train around, so he slid one hand up to the back of her head and took possession of her mouth.

His cock jumped to attention immediately because she moaned against his lips. The kiss went from zero to ten in seconds, switching from a sweet taste to an insistent urgency neither of them could stop.

Tavis's heart raced as he slid his tongue along the slit of her lips to demand entrance, and he gripped her with his fingers when she granted his wish.

Another moan filled the air, but he wasn't sure if it was him or her this time. It didn't matter.

She leaned into him, crushing her body to his, causing him to stumble backward until his ass hit the counter. Her hands roamed around to the back of his neck and his shoulders, exploring everywhere she could reach while he stroked her tongue and tasted every inch of her mouth.

When they came up for air, it was out of necessity. He needed to breathe. She did too.

"Well, that answers that question," she panted.

"Yeah. And raises about ten others." He closed his eyes and looked toward the ceiling. *Now what?*

"Please tell me you don't have a woman somewhere back home. I've never asked."

"Of course not." He rubbed her back absently and set his chin on the top of her head. "I haven't been in one place long enough to develop a relationship in years. You're the one with a string of suitors," he joked, intentionally using the stilted word rich people used.

She groaned and tipped her head back again. "None that matter. You know that, right?"

"Yes." He smoothed a hand around to cup her face, stroking her jaw with his thumb. "I was joking."

"We need to slow this ship down, don't we?" she asked.

"Yes."

"That's going to be hard," she pointed out.

"Very." He smiled at her to make sure she knew without a doubt that he cared. That he was attracted to her. That he wanted her.

She released him and backed up a few steps, glancing around. "I guess we should clean this mess up. Are you going to call the police?"

"No. Not unless you think something's missing."

She shook her head. "Nothing. It's just a mess."

"That might have been the only intention. For someone to make sure we know they're aware of where you're staying and that they're watching you."

She sighed and tucked her fingertips in her jeans pockets. "Surely you don't think it was someone who knows me?"

He reached for her to stroke her cheek again. "Not taking any chances, hon. Your days of keeping me a secret just ended."

She cocked her head to one side and gave him a strange look he couldn't quite read. "How close do you intend to stay? Am I going to need to slide to one side of my bed?"

"Yes." He didn't hesitate. He also didn't smile or laugh. This was serious. He wouldn't sleep in another room and leave her vulnerable.

Her eyes shot up, as did her lips. "Winning."

He rolled his eyes and groaned. "Keep your hands to yourself, evil woman. I'm not getting under the covers with you. Just planning to stay closer." He glanced around. "Let's clean this up, then I'll call your father, then we need to get some sleep."

It took thirty minutes to put things mostly back to rights before Tavis sat on the couch and dialed her father. He had a private cell number that would surpass any secret service or secretaries who ordinarily screened the man's calls.

"Hello?" The secretary of state answered on the second ring.

"Sir, this is Tavis Neade."

Colette took a seat next to Tavis, facing him.

"Mr. Neade. Yes. Is everything okay with my daughter? Please tell me she hasn't given you the slip." The man wasn't laughing. He was serious.

"No. She's perfectly safe and right next to me. I just wanted to let you know there was a break-in at her apartment. We weren't here at the time. Nothing seems to be missing. Nothing broken. Just ransacked as if they were either looking for something or wanted to leave their calling card."

"Shit. Don't suppose you could talk her into coming home?"

"No, sir." Tavis didn't hesitate. The fastest way he could cause Colette to give him the slip would be to tell her she had to go home. "I don't think she's in imminent danger. I won't let her out of my sight. Let's hope it was a coincidence. But I promise she is safe with me."

Colette leaned her head against Tavis's biceps. She could undoubtedly hear her father.

Mr. Loughlin sighed loudly, taking a few seconds before continuing. "I appreciate you letting me know. Please keep her safe. That's my main priority. And if anything else happens, I want you to talk her into leaving."

"I'll do what I can, sir. Is there anything I should know that you haven't shared with my team yet? Any past threats that weren't resolved? And current threats you haven't mentioned?"

"No. You know everything I know. I just like my daughter to be safe."

"I can understand that, sir. And she is safe. I won't let a thing happen to her." He gripped her thigh and squeezed.

"Thank you, Mr. Neade."

"Please, call me Tavis."

"Okay. Tavis. Keep me posted."

"Will do. Have a good day, sir."

The moment the connection ended, Colette leaned back and sighed deeply. "Thank you."

"For what?"

"For helping me stay here. He can be pretty persuasive."

Tavis turned his body to fully face her and slid a hand to her neck. "I meant what I said. You aren't out of my sight except to pee. Got it? And even then, I want to be on the other side of the door. If we're at the university, I'll check the bathroom out first."

She nodded. "Okay." Her voice was soft. "But only because I happen to like you. If you were someone else, I would sneak away later tonight and run for freedom."

He lifted a brow. "Do I need to get the handcuffs out?"

She flushed.

My God. She was so fucking cute. He couldn't resist grabbing her wrist and encircling it with his fingers. "I can and will cuff this arm to the bedframe if you give me any reason not to trust you." He was half kidding. But the other half of him wished she would give him even the smallest reason to act on his threat. He could picture her panting against the mattress, driven mad with arousal from being restrained.

Not every woman would react that way. Most wouldn't. But the way Colette was licking her lips, her cheeks rosy, her eyes wide, and her body trembling... Yeah, she was aroused. "What if I like the idea?" she murmured.

He groaned and stood, pulling her alongside him. "Go shower. I'll be right behind you," he said to change the subject.

She lifted both brows. "You'll be right behind me coming into the shower?" she taunted.

"No, imp. I'll be behind you coming upstairs. I'm going to make sure the door is secured. Tomorrow, I'm going to add a second lock and an alarm."

"How did they get in?" she asked, glancing at the door.

"No forced entry. They picked the lock."

She nodded slowly. "That's kind of freaky."

"Yes, it is. That's why you're not getting out of my sight. Please, promise me you aren't going to fight me on this issue."

"I won't. I promise. I told you I won't, and I meant it."

"Okay." He released her and pointed at the stairs. "Shower. Now." He needed her to get out of his space before he grabbed her around the waist and flattened her to the sofa.

Tavis could usually keep himself in check in any circumstances, but he was quickly realizing there was no way he could defend himself against Colette's advances much longer.

He didn't even want to.

CHAPTER 8

Colette's hands were shaking as she took her shower. She couldn't remember if she'd put conditioner in or not before realizing instead she'd washed her hair twice.

Her brain was completely focused on one thing. Tavis. The way his hands had felt in her hair and on her back. The way he'd held her against him as if he needed to pull her tighter so he wouldn't lose her. The way he kissed her like they hadn't seen each other for years and would soon be parted again.

She'd fought this attraction for days. For two weeks. She'd tried to deny it, and she knew he had too. They were failing. It was over. He would be in her space constantly now. She was both glad and nervous at the same time.

How the hell was she going to share a bed with him and not jump his bones? She would be humiliated if she tried to make a pass at him and got rejected. There would be no way she could face him the next day.

She needed to rein in her arousal, which was hard while running her hands up and down her body through the slippery soap. Was he standing outside the bathroom door?

Probably. Which meant she couldn't stroke herself to orgasm without him knowing. She wasn't quiet enough for that.

When she turned the water off, she was feeling more desperate than before the shower. On top of that, she'd entered the bathroom without anything to wear. *Shit.*

She took her time combing her long hair out, putting on moisturizer, brushing her teeth. Finally, she had nothing left to do and opened the door wearing nothing but the towel wrapped around her.

Tavis was sitting on the edge of her bed. He looked up and swallowed. "Hey."

She pointed toward her dresser. "Forgot to bring in pajamas," she mumbled before drawing in a deep breath and meeting his gaze. "Actually, I don't own pajamas."

He lifted both brows and then rubbed his forehead with two fingers. "You did mention you were going to sleep virtually naked that first night. I wasn't sure you were serious."

"Well…yeah."

"Okay, not tonight." He pushed to standing and headed for the door. "Put something on. Anything. I don't care what. I'll wait in the hall."

She watched as he rushed out of the room and shut the door as if fire was chasing him. In a way it was cute. She might have laughed if this situation weren't so serious.

She padded across the room, yanked open a drawer, and grabbed panties and a T-shirt. She didn't own anything that would totally cover her ass, but this would have to do. After hurrying back into the bathroom to hang up her towel and put on the meager clothing, she scrambled into the bed and under the covers.

This entire dance was unnecessary. She should have simply dropped the towel, pushed the issue, and put an end to their awkwardness. It was only a matter of time before they ended up in bed together. Why bother to put off the inevitable?

She cleared her throat. "Tavis?"

He opened the door slowly until he saw her under the covers and then came fully into the room. The man was wearing loose sweatpants and a T-shirt. He flipped off the light before coming over to her side of the bed.

For a moment, she held her breath, wondering why he was heading straight toward her, but then he reached over her head and unfastened the mosquito netting. *Duh*.

After releasing all four corners, he lowered himself onto the opposite side of the bed and sighed as soon as his head hit the pillow. There was just enough light coming from outside for her to watch him rubbing his temples again as she rolled to face him.

"I hate this awkwardness," she murmured.

He turned toward her, leaving several inches of space between them. "We have chemistry. It's undeniable. But—"

"Why must we add a 'but' to it? It's been two weeks. We're stuck together for six months. That's a long time. How long do you think we can keep our hands off each other?" Bold words coming from her, but she meant them.

He smirked. "About one more day probably, but humor me so I can take that day to think."

She stared at him, taking in his expression—half serious, half humored. "And this will accomplish what? Do you think you can talk yourself out of climbing *under* the covers between now and this time tomorrow?" she taunted.

He chuckled. "Doubt it, temptress."

She slowly smiled.

"What's that look for?" he asked, brow furrowed, grin still in place.

"My new nickname? Trading princess for temptress? I think I like it."

He groaned and dropped onto his back to stare at the ceiling.

A loud crash followed by an animal squealing made both of them sit upright.

Colette gasped. *What the fuck was that?* "Tavis?" she whispered loudly, heart pounding.

He jumped to his feet, grabbed a gun from the bedside table next to him, and moved silently and swiftly toward the bedroom door. He glanced back. "Don't move, Colette."

She nodded. She was too scared to move an inch anyway. "Be careful," she mouthed, though she doubted he heard her. Suddenly, for the first time in her life, she was glad to have a bodyguard.

She wished he hadn't shut the door behind him as he headed down the stairs because she couldn't hear a thing. All she could do was sit there, fisting the sheets, panicking, eyes wide and pinned to the door, ears straining to hear any sound at all.

Seconds ticked by that seemed like minutes. A door shut. She thought it was the front door. Did he leave? He wouldn't go outside, would he? This wasn't a horror film where the hero hears a noise and heads toward the danger.

Finally, she heard his footsteps on the stairs and he was back in the room, shutting the door again and rushing to her side.

He set the gun on her bedside table and sat next to her before grabbing her shoulders. "It's okay. It was the neighbor's cat. He must have come in the front door while it was ajar and we didn't see him. He knocked the lamp off the end table. It must have scared him to death. I shooed him back outside and locked us in tight."

"A cat?" She was struggling to absorb all of this.

"Seriously? And you think it scared *him*? What about us?" She was shaking.

Tavis tipped his head back and forth. "Well, all of us, yes. You okay?" He slid his hands up and down her biceps.

She shook her head. "Nope. Not even close. That cat stole eight of my nine lives."

Tavis nodded. "Not going to lie. I was freaked out too."

"No. You're not allowed to freak out. You're the bodyguard. Don't tell me shit like that."

He gave her a lopsided smile. "Well, I don't mean I was exactly scared for my life or yours so much as concerned about your fear. I knew you were scared."

She drew in a deep breath. He was right. "See?"

"See what?" he asked, brows coming together.

"Life is short. You never know what's going to happen. We should probably go ahead and have sex. What if one of us gets hit by a boda-boda tomorrow?"

He chuckled. "Nice try. I promise I'm good at my job. We'll both live through tomorrow. I'll look both ways to make sure no motorcycle is in our path." He leaned forward as if to kiss her forehead, but she tipped her head back and brought her lips to his instead, causing him to kiss her full on the mouth.

It was underhanded, but it worked. Tavis gripped her arms tighter as he tipped his head to one side and deepened the kiss, consuming her like he had earlier. The same fireworks went off. It hadn't been a fluke.

Eventually, he jerked back, breaking the connection with a groan. "Temptress," he grumbled.

"Is it working?" she breathed.

"Yes." But he followed that word up by rising and releasing her to round to the other side of the bed. He dropped down hard on his back, making the entire bed bounce. His chest was rising and falling as he tossed an arm over his eyes.

She twisted to face him, staring down at him, waiting. When he didn't say a word or move a single muscle other than the rise and fall of his deep breaths, she finally cleared her throat. "Tavis?"

"Give me a second, hon." His voice was soft, controlled.

She nodded even though he couldn't see her. She wasn't playing fair. How could she tell him stories about how she'd hit on previous bodyguards for the fun of it to annoy them and then do essentially the same thing to him? He couldn't even know for sure if she was serious or just a raving bitch. He probably suspected the latter.

Finally, she slid back under the covers and lowered her head to the pillow, facing him. "I'm sorry. I shouldn't have done that. It wasn't fair. I won't do it again."

He dropped his arm and rolled toward her, his hand coming up to cup her face. His thumb grazed over her cheek. "No reason to be sorry, and it will totally happen again. And you're not alone in this attraction. Don't read me wrong."

"Okay," she murmured.

"I need you to understand that sleeping with you puts me in a difficult position. Technically, I could get fired."

She widened her eyes. "How the hell would my dad know we were sleeping together?"

"I'm not talking about your dad. I'm talking about my bosses at Holt. I'm not in the habit of lying to them. They're my friends. My teammates from the SEALs. We don't keep secrets, least of all about women. They would haul my ass home and replace me before the sun set if I told them I'm attracted to you."

"Oh." *Well, shit.*

"And the truth is I don't want to leave you here with

someone else. I'm uneasy about your situation. Hopefully my gut is wrong, but something is crawling up my spine that's got me on edge."

She licked her lips. "You think I'm really in danger?" She'd never really believed that at any point. Not even last week when... She shook the reminder from her head, not wanting to discuss what happened last week.

Richard Tillerman. The son of a wealthy banker. A man her parents wholeheartedly approved of and had pressured her to date. If they only knew what a smarmy piece of shit the guy was.

She didn't honestly believe Richard Tillerman was a danger to her, and discussing his constant advances would be embarrassing. Tavis would want to hear every detail, which would open a can of worms she wasn't interested in opening.

Colette shook Richard from her mind and focused on Tavis as he answered her. "I don't know. Something just feels off, hon. I don't usually get this rattled. Maybe it's because I care about you, but I think it's more than that. I can't put my finger on it."

"You think the break-in..."

He shrugged. "Don't know. Could be random. Lots of things could be random."

She closed her eyes and enjoyed the feel of him touching her.

He leaned in closer, so close she could feel his warm breath on her face, smell his minty toothpaste. "I need you to be safe. I can't keep you safe if I'm distracted by climbing under the covers and following my dick."

She met his gaze. "I get it." *I don't like it, but I get it.*

He kissed her gently and pulled back. "Do not misread me, Colette. I'm into you. Make no mistake. It's wrong on so many levels, but it's true. Let me protect you. Hold your temptress side at bay for a bit, okay?" He gave her that damn half grin again.

She sighed. "Okay."

"Thank you." He gave her yet another quick kiss and backed off, releasing her. "Go to sleep."

"Sure," she murmured. As if that were an option right now. Her heart was racing. Her nipples were stiff. If he weren't in the bed, she would absolutely masturbate to take the edge off. So, to add insult to injury, not only was he going to keep his hands to himself, but he was forcing her to do the same.

Ugh. She dropped onto her back and took several deep breaths.

He chuckled.

She jerked her head in his direction. "What's so funny?"

"You are, temptress."

She groaned and rolled away from him, pulling her knees up and plumping her pillow. *Damn infuriating man.*

CHAPTER 9

"Tell me you've got something useful for me," Tavis demanded when he connected with Ryker on Wednesday afternoon.

Colette was in a lab where she'd be working for another few hours. He'd scoped the area out many times. There was only one way in and out of the room, so he felt confident walking a distance away as long as he could still see the door.

"I wish I had more," Ryker informed him. "Still haven't located Steve Lacoste. That doesn't mean a damn thing of course. Just because the man is in the wind doesn't mean he's hunting down Colette. It's been years since she dodged that bullet, getting him fired."

Tavis kept his gaze locked on the lab door while he spoke. "I'm keeping him near the top of the list of possible threats since he can't be located and he harassed her."

"Okay, but keep in mind, your list is based on a gut feeling. You have no way of knowing there's any actual threat against her life."

Tavis sighed. "Something is off. I can feel it in my bones."

"You still think her dad knows something he isn't telling us?"

"I do." Tavis shuddered. He'd gotten a weird vibe from the man when he'd spoken to him on the phone.

"But why would William Loughlin withhold information that puts his only daughter in danger? That's risky," Ryker pointed out.

Tavis nodded slowly, his gaze on the door as someone entered the lab. He recognized the guy from previous days. Isaac Sorter. A fellow PhD candidate. He was no threat to Colette. He might get his heart broken when she never returned his obvious affections, but that was about it for Isaac.

Tavis ran a hand through his hair, forcing himself not to feel jealous of Isaac. Yes, the guy got to spend hours upon hours with Colette. Yes, the man could also converse with her about a subject she was passionate about—a subject Tavis couldn't begin to entertain her with. And yes, Isaac turned on the charm every time he was with her while Tavis watched.

However, Colette clearly didn't return the affection. She spoke to Isaac politely, nodding and grinning when appropriate, but she also maintained a closed-off stance, arms crossed keeping space between them. Feeling jealous would be absurd. Colette made it perfectly clear she was into Tavis.

Not that he'd done a thing about it. Yet. Nor should he. Other than kiss her. He hadn't even done that again since Sunday night. She'd stopped tempting him, and he'd kept his distance. It wouldn't last forever, but the longer he could put off climbing between her legs the better.

"Tavis?" Ryker inquired.

"Oh, sorry. I was distracted."

"Uh huh. Is there anything I need to know?" Ryker asked.

Tavis cringed. There was no way he could keep Ryker and Ajax from knowing about his attraction to Colette much longer either. "About what?"

"You seem overly concerned about Colette's safety."

Tavis straightened his spine. "That's absurd. It's my job. Isn't her safety what I was hired for?"

"Of course, but other than a break-in at her apartment, which you yourself admitted could have been random, the rest of your suspicions are based on hunches."

Tavis gritted his teeth and then drew in a deep breath. "You and Ajax have agreed from the beginning that something is off about this assignment," Tavis pointed out.

"True, but I'm not sure I'd be going to great lengths to dig so thoroughly into every hunch. We've found nothing yet. It's reasonable to assume her father is simply overprotective. He has been for most of her life."

"Maybe." Tavis chewed on the inside of his cheek. Was he overreacting?

Ryker sighed. "You're into her, aren't you?"

Tavis held his breath. *Fuck.*

"Aha. Is this going to affect your ability to do your job?"

"No," he responded quickly.

"Are you sleeping with her?" Ryker's voice was calm. Not accusatory or even angry. Just inquisitive. Which Tavis appreciated.

"No." He cleared his throat and admitted, "Not yet."

"But you'd like to be."

"Yes. I'm trying to be professional."

"Does she feel the same way?"

"Yes."

Ryker groaned.

"Before you get any big ideas, no, I don't want you to replace me. I wouldn't be able to leave her. I'd lose my mind turning her over to someone else's care. It's out of the question. I need you to trust me to do my job and keep my head on straight." He was asking a lot. He knew it. Ryker had every right to pull Tavis off the job this very minute.

"You know damn good and well any member of our team would lay down his life for her. Don't act like Gramps, Keebler, Pitbull, Viper, or Loki couldn't do as good a job as you, if not better."

Tavis stiffened. "I don't like your implication."

"You *resemble* my implication, Bones." His voice rose, still not in anger, but to make a point. "I've been in your shoes. I know what you're feeling. Don't forget I was on assignment with Xena hunting your ass down in Ethiopia. I know *exactly* what it's like to fall for the woman I'm working with."

Tavis wanted to argue this was different. Colette wasn't his coworker. She was someone he'd been assigned to protect. But he knew he'd be arguing semantics if he pointed that out.

"Is your head in the game, Bones?"

"Yes."

"If that changes, I expect you to let me know immediately. Don't you fucking let your guard down with her. I know I spent the first part of this conversation pointing out that maybe there is no real legit threat against Colette Loughlin, but we both know I could be wrong. There's just as much chance someone *is* after her. I need to know I can count on you to do your job."

"You can. You know you can. No matter what, she's safe with me."

Ryker sighed.

Tavis continued, "You also know I could have lied to you and told you I didn't want something more from Colette. But I didn't lie. I told you the truth. Please respect me enough in return to make the best decisions where her life is concerned."

"Okay." Ryker's voice was calmer. "Okay," he repeated.

"Check another angle for me," Tavis requested, changing the subject.

"Give it to me."

"Dig around and see if you can find any dirt on Secretary Loughlin."

Ryker sighed audibly through the phone. "Already on it."

"Thanks. I hope I'm wrong, but he wouldn't be the first or the last powerful man to have something going down on the side that put him at risk for blackmail."

"Let's touch base again in a few days."

"Sounds good." Tavis ended the call but continued to stand where he was, watching the exit to the lab. So far, no one had realized he was assigned to Colette, and he considered that a win for her. Since it was important to her. He hadn't expected to go more than a few days keeping his assignment to protect her a secret from her classmates, but it had now been over two weeks. Either no one had noticed him or they chose not to say anything to her.

A few minutes later, several students filed out of the lab, including Colette who was talking to Isaac.

Tavis tried not to react to Isaac having Colette's undivided attention. It was natural. Isaac was a colleague. They shared a similar interest and knowledge base. A subject matter Tavis would never know enough about to carry on a conversation.

An unreasonable sensation crawled up his spine as he

watched Colette nod and smile at whatever Isaac was saying. Tavis wasn't up to her standards. He didn't have an advanced degree. He may have been a Navy SEAL, but as far as her coworkers would be concerned, he would be nothing more than a bodyguard when they caught on to the ruse.

Why did that unnerve him so much? It shouldn't. And he should remember how incompatible the two of them were the next time he adjusted his straining cock. Pursuing her was incredibly irresponsible. He would never fit into her social circle.

Hell, her father would have a coronary if he had any idea the kind of thoughts running through Tavis's mind. None of them were pure. That was for sure.

Jeez. Tavis rubbed his forehead as he watched Colette continue to speak to Isaac. He narrowed his gaze and considered approaching when he saw her cross her arms and take a step back. She was still smiling, but it was forced now. What had Isaac said to her?

Tavis took a step closer but then stopped himself. She was fine. No need to interfere. A few moments later, she looked around, found Tavis, pointed at him, and then waved.

Isaac's eyes widened as he spotted Tavis. He blinked a few times and then jerked his gaze back to Colette. He was visibly shaking and took a slow step back, increasing the space between himself and Colette.

That's right, buddy. She's mine.

Tavis shook the ridiculous thought from his head. Could he be any more of a caveman? Thank God he hadn't said that out loud. Or in front of Colette.

It hadn't been a full minute since he'd reminded himself he wasn't right for her, and here he was mentally fist pumping whatever was going on between her and Isaac for no good reason.

Finally, Isaac waved awkwardly at her and turned to rush off in the opposite direction.

Colette came toward Tavis. She was already rolling her eyes as she approached. "Your head is so large it's a wonder you're able to hold it up over your shoulders," she teased as she reached him.

He ignored her and glanced back toward the lab. "What was that all about?"

"He asked me out. I had to think quick, so I told him I had a boyfriend."

Tavis lifted both brows. That was even better than he'd expected.

She licked her lips. "I know that was overstepping and irresponsible. I shouldn't have said it. Now I'm stuck pretending you're my boyfriend for months. Are you mad?"

He was certain his brows lifted even higher. "Mad? No. Why would I be mad? Makes my job easier." *And keeps me from having to confront would-be suitors.*

He reached out and slid his hand under the strap of her backpack to slide it off her shoulder.

"What are you doing?"

"Carrying your books. That's what boyfriends do."

She rolled her eyes again and jerked out of reach. "Not mine. My boyfriends treat me as an equal who's capable of carrying my own luggage and books."

"And how many of these boyfriends have you had?"

She groaned and stepped past him, heading for the SUV.

He took two strides to catch up to her, grabbed the back of her pack, and gave a little tug to halt her progress.

Leaning over her shoulder, he asked, "How many?" He pressured her purely to fuel his ego for no good reason.

"You already know the answer," she grumbled. She spun around to face him and met his gaze. "Don't get all cocky on me. Just because I haven't had a long-term boyfriend doesn't mean I haven't dated. I'm not a virgin. Nor am I some wilting flower."

Okay then. That answered his next burning question. He hadn't really thought much about her amount of experience until now, but if she hadn't had a boyfriend at all then it was a logical possibility.

Tavis slid his hand down her arm and threaded their fingers together. "Am I permitted to hold your hand, temptress?"

"Of course." She glanced back toward the lab. "No one will believe you're my boyfriend if you don't." She gave him a fake grin.

He narrowed his gaze, stepped closer, and tipped her chin back. "How much of this is fake, Colette?"

She swallowed. "I don't know."

He nodded slowly. "Okay."

"You're the one keeping me at arm's length. Sleeping next to me night after night in my bed without touching me. You tell me when it's no longer fake."

He stared at her for a long time, ten thousand concerns eating at him. Finally, he turned toward the path and tugged her in the direction of the car. This little game they were playing was serious. He needed to get his head on straight and be careful before one or both of them got hurt.

The truth was he really liked her. He'd tried to ignore his feelings for the last several days, but his feelings hadn't diminished. He found himself watching her more than necessary to keep her safe.

His favorite time to watch her was when she was

sleeping. She was so peaceful and sexy. The temptress slept in a T-shirt and panties. Sometimes she kicked off the damn covers and gave him far too much of a show.

He'd seen her panties from the front and the back. The woman had fucking amazing taste in lingerie too. Sexy lace panties in every color. He also knew she shaved her pussy because he'd gotten a close enough look several times.

And her butt. Jesus. Her ass was fine. Tight and round and tempting like the woman it belonged to. He wanted to cup it with his hands and squeeze.

He didn't meet Colette's gaze when they reached the SUV. He simply took her bag, tossed it in the back seat, and helped her into the vehicle.

The drive home was silent, though he was aware of her staring at him. He wasn't sure how to handle this situation. He needed to man up and make a decision and fast. His head told him to nip this in the bud, tell her they couldn't be a couple under no uncertain terms. His heart was screaming at him to flatten her to the wall as soon as they entered the apartment and ravage her.

By the time they got home, he was even more wound up. He let them in, reset the alarm, and set their bags on the sofa.

When he turned around, Colette was in his face, flattening her palms on his chest. "Talk to me. Are you mad that I told Isaac we were a couple? I can undo that easily enough. I can tell him we broke up or something if you want. I shouldn't have made that decision without speaking to you first. I wasn't thinking. I just said the first thing that came to mind when he asked me out."

Tavis shook his head and slid his hands up her arms to her shoulders. "No. I'm not mad. I was jealous of Isaac to be honest. It wasn't rational, but I was. When he glanced at me with that deer-in-the-headlights look, I suspected you'd told him something along that line. I did a silent fist pump."

Colette smiled. "Good. Then it's settled."

He narrowed his gaze. "What's settled? I don't think anything is settled. You belong with a man like Isaac. Not someone like me." There. He'd said it.

Her eyes went wide. "Are you fucking kidding me right now?"

"No. He's intellectual. He'll stimulate your mind. You get excited when you discuss epidemiology with other people. I can't give you that. I'm—"

She reached up and flattened her palm against his lips. "Don't you dare fucking go there, Tavis. Do not finish that sentence. Are you shitting me? Isaac? You think I need his kind of intellectual stimulation to be happy?"

Tavis lifted his brows. He couldn't respond. Not easily. Her hand was still clamped over his lips.

"I go to classes and work in the lab nearly every day of the week. I get all the intellectual stimulation I need when I'm there. No one in that lab or any of those classes makes my panties wet or my nipples stiffen. That's all you. And it matters more than anything."

He stared at her for a moment and then grabbed her hand and tugged it away from his mouth.

She pressed her body against his. All of her body. Enough that she couldn't miss the rock-solid erection nestled against her belly. Her voice dropped when she spoke again. "Evidence would suggest you're just as attracted to me. We've already been around this block. I get why you've held yourself at arm's length. It's messy. It's complicated. It's ten other things. The list is long. But it's happening anyway."

He was breathing heavily as if he'd jogged down the block to get to her. "Temptress," he teased, smiling. He was still gripping her fingers and he brought them to his lips to kiss her knuckles one at a time. "When your father finds out about this, he's going to fire me."

"Who's going to tell him?" She lifted a brow.

He groaned. She had a point. But he wasn't really interested in a one-night stand with Colette. Nor was he interested in one week or one month. This was serious. Maybe she didn't see it that way. Maybe for her this was a fling. "I think we need to have a come-to-Jesus chat, Colette."

"Why do we need to invite Jesus? We're dancing around each other every day. How long are we going to do that? How long can you sleep next to me at night and not touch me? How long are you going to watch my every move with that scowl on your face and not act on it? How long, Tavis?"

He slid his free hand around to the small of her back. "I have a how-long question for you too, temptress. How long do you see this lasting?"

"How the fuck should I know? It hasn't even started yet and you want an end date?" Her voice rose.

"Temptress, it started the moment we met, and you know it. And no, I don't want an end date. That's the problem."

She blinked at him. "What are you saying?"

"I'm saying I'm really into you, Colette. I'm not interested in a quick fuck. I don't want to be your Uganda man. If you can't see me in your life, cut me loose now."

The blinking switched to staring. "Oh."

"Yeah. Oh." He held his breath, half expecting her to turn and walk away. Maybe he'd asked for too much. But he needed to be firm. This was important. Not just because she had the power to break his heart but because he needed to work with her for five more months. It would be ugly if she ended things.

"Wow."

This wasn't going well. Tavis eased her away from him.

Colette stopped him, grabbing his shoulders and sliding her arms up around his neck. "Don't misread me. I'm not saying *no*. I'm just surprised."

"Why would it surprise you that I'm into you?"

"Because no one's ever been interested in me like this before. I mean, men have pretended to be for their own personal gain, but no one serious. I'm processing. Give me a second." Her chest was rising and falling. In a few moments she said, "Really?" Her voice hitched.

He chuckled. "Yes, temptress. Really. If you can't see something long-term with me, don't fuck with my head."

"I've never fucked with anyone's head before, Tavis. It's not my style."

He slid his hands up her back. "I know. That didn't come out right. I just want you to think about things a bit."

Her mouth opened and then closed before opening again. "So, you're saying there's actually a man alive who would put off having sex because he cares enough to want more?"

"That's what I'm saying." He smirked. "Gotta say, I'm rather surprised myself. It's not just because I'm some kind of perfect gentleman. It's also because your life could be at stake here, Colette. I won't take a risk with your life. We don't really know what we're facing. If I'm going to climb *under* the covers with you instead of holding vigil on top, I'll only be able to protect you if I'm sure I'll be staying there."

She nodded slowly. "Makes sense. Though it does seem you're some robotic gentleman, I've got to say."

He smirked. "I'm not. Or at least I wasn't before I met

you." He brought his lips to hers and kissed her, keeping it light. Sweet.

"You're not going to have sex with me tonight," she pointed out.

"Nope."

"Ugh. I'm going to develop a complex."

He chuckled. "I'm going to develop blue balls."

"Whose fault is that?"

"Mine and mine alone." He slid his hands down and cupped her ass, something he'd wanted to do for weeks, and damn, it felt as fine as he'd expected. Better.

CHAPTER 10

"You're putting a cramp in my style, SEAL."

"How's that?" She loved the way he gave her a lopsided grin.

"At least when you were sleeping across the hall from me in another room, I could pull out my vibrator, close my eyes, and pretend it was you making me come at night. Now that you're sleeping in my bed—or rather *on* my bed—I haven't had an orgasm in far too many days," she admitted.

He swallowed hard. "Jesus, temptress." He dropped his forehead against hers and groaned. "You're going to kill me."

She shook her head against his. "I'm going to be the one dying. From lack of orgasms. I bet you get to orgasm every day. Shower? Bathroom? It's not that easy for me. I can't get myself off in two minutes in the shower with my fingers."

She knew she was oversharing. But dammit, she was also telling the truth. She no longer cared if she was tempting him. She wasn't even embarrassed. The man brought something out of her she'd never been aware of before. She felt open to talk to him about anything, including sex. Including her fucking horny needs.

Tavis growled before he grabbed her hand and headed for the stairs. He hauled her along behind him until they reached the edge of her bed. When they arrived, he squared off in front of her, cupped her face, and kissed her like his life depended on it.

In seconds she was putty, melting against him, her hands on his ass, sliding into his jeans' pockets. She forgot everything. The world ceased to exist while she kissed him back just as passionately.

When he broke the kiss, he was panting, his gaze locked on hers, his face close, his hands still holding her face. "I'll make dinner. Take your time."

Her brows lifted high. "What? *No.*" She shook her head. "No way."

"Why not?"

"It doesn't work like that, Tavis. There's no way I could masturbate alone in my bedroom with you knowing it and standing downstairs. Or how would I know you weren't right outside the bedroom listening?" She shook her head all during this speech. "Nice gesture, but no."

Tavis drew in a deep breath and closed his eyes before meeting her gaze again. "Okay, *I'll* do it."

"What?" She was confused. *He'll do what?* But she wasn't confused for long because his hands were on her shirt, which he drew up over her head before tackling the button on her jeans.

Holy shit. He was going to give her an orgasm?

No. No way. She grabbed his hands. "Tavis…"

He shrugged off her fumbling fingers and batted them away.

"*Tavis.*" Her voice was higher pitched, ringing in the room. "I can't."

He paused, her button open, her zipper down.

She gasped, her knees threatening to give out. *Fuck. Maybe I can.*

His hand flattened on her belly and slid down into her panties.

Her breath hitched when he found her pussy and then stroked her clit. "You can't what, temptress?"

"I…" The one syllable was breathless, and she forgot what she was going to say as he pushed a finger up into her, causing her to lift off the floor onto her toes.

Her head rolled back.

He tugged her jeans over her hips with his other hand, mumbling, "Tell me, temptress. What can't you do?" He added another finger, and she grabbed his biceps to keep from falling as he penetrated her.

"C-come."

"You can't come?" he whispered in her ear. "Why not?"

"Mmm." It would seem she could come. He was about to rock her world and change everything. It unnerved her.

She grabbed his hand, pressing against it, not pulling him out, but forcing him to still for a moment. She met his gaze. She was panting. "No one's ever made me come, Tavis," she breathed. "I've never come with someone else in the room."

He drew in a sharp breath and then nodded once. "That's about to change."

She moaned when he removed his hand, trembling with need. Not only did she not come with men but she didn't come this fast. This easily. "Tavis…" What the hell was his plan?

He squatted down to remove her shoes and then yanked off her jeans and then her panties so fast her head was spinning. Seconds later, he was standing again, but he had a hand between her breasts and one at her back. He gave her a shove so that she fell onto the mattress, but controlled the pace.

"Tavis," she cried out when he pushed her knees apart and stared at her pussy.

He lifted his gaze to hers. "So fucking sexy. So wet and hot and swollen for me. I'm going to use my mouth, okay? I need to taste you."

She licked her lips while he waited for her to consent. She swallowed. This was important. "Okay, but you're going to ruin me, so you better have meant every word you said earlier. Don't you dare take this from me and then turn away from me."

She was panting, struggling to get enough oxygen.

Tavis slid his palms down her inner thighs, making her moan at the intimacy. He parted her lower lips, tormenting her further. She'd never been this desperate, not even with her vibrator and her imagination.

He surprised her when he leaned over and kissed her lips reverently. "You're mine, temptress."

All she could do was nod as he lowered his mouth to her chest to kiss the upper swell of her breasts before reaching under the edge of lace to flick his tongue over a nipple.

She fisted the covers at her sides and moaned, her head tipping back, her chest arching. *Holy shit.*

He did the same to her other nipple before kissing a path down her stomach. After a long deep inhale that made her shudder, he closed his mouth over her clit and sucked.

Colette cried out incoherently, her entire body stiffening.

Nothing had ever felt like that before. She'd never

dreamed it could feel that good. When he flicked his tongue over her clit and then speared it into her, she arched farther. "Tavis," she screamed.

He thrust a finger into her and then another, sucking on her clit at the same time.

She writhed, unable to remain still. She released the covers to grab his shoulders. It was impossible to ground herself. She felt like she was going to fall apart, float away. The pieces of her would scatter around the room.

When he curled his fingers up to graze over the soft spongy spot at the top of her channel and dragged his teeth over her clit, she screamed, her orgasm slamming into her, pulsing with so much force that her entire body shook with the vibrations.

Tavis knew what he was doing. The man was an expert with his mouth. He knew exactly when to ease up the pressure right before her clit would have been too sensitive to tolerate his tongue anymore.

He didn't back off though. While she gasped, trying to catch her breath, he nibbled all over her pussy, licking and sucking gently. He continued to hold her thighs wide. Finally, he planted one final kiss on her mound and lifted his head.

He was grinning. "You can't come with a man?"

She groaned. "You'll never let that go, will you?"

"No, temptress. Never. Not for the rest of our lives."

She shivered at the mention of forever. Could this thing really be forever? It seemed crazy and preposterous and possible and right at the same time. Her brain couldn't process all these feelings.

"You're fully clothed," she pointed out.

"Yep. Gonna stay that way too."

"Why?"

He shrugged. "Like you said, I can and yes, I have masturbated every day since I met you. I hate that you have not. From now on, take some time for yourself every day. Lock the bathroom door. Take baths while I fix dinner."

She gasped. "After that?" She shook her head. "I'm spoiled now. Ruined. I doubt if my vibrator will even work anymore," she half joked.

He chuckled, his head cocking to one side before he tapped her cheek. "You're flushed. Does it embarrass you to masturbate in the bathroom while I'm downstairs?"

"Yes." No reason to lie. "Absolutely."

"But it doesn't embarrass you for me to strip you down and eat your sweet pussy?" He was teasing her.

She groaned. "It happened so fast I didn't even know what was going on. Before I knew it, I was naked and you were fucking me with your tongue, Tavis. I didn't have time to be embarrassed." Now that he mentioned it, she probably would be slightly mortified when she found all her scattered brain cells.

He slid his hands up to her bra, unfastened the clasp between her breasts, and parted the sides.

She shivered, her nipples stiffening further as the air hit them, if that was possible.

Tavis reverently cupped both sides and leaned over to kiss first one nipple and then the other. "You're so fucking gorgeous," he murmured.

"You're not so bad yourself. I bet you're even better naked," she tempted.

He chuckled before releasing her entirely. "Be right back."

She was stunned when he turned and left the room, and she rose up onto her elbows, feeling decidedly naked and self-conscious.

Seconds later he was back, and he was holding up one of his T-shirts. "From now on, you'll sleep in mine instead of yours." He lifted it over her head. It dwarfed her.

"Why?" she asked as she snatched her panties out of his hand. He'd picked them up off the floor, and she had to draw the line at him putting them back on her.

"Because yours don't cover your sweet ass, temptress, which drives me bonkers in the middle of the night."

She grinned. "Is that so?" *Good to know.*

"Yes." He backed up. "Dinner. I'll go get it started." And then he spun and bolted from the room.

His ass was fine even encased in his jeans, but damn, she wished he would have let her see more of him. She was at a tremendous disadvantage. She always had been, especially since she slept in very little clothing and now knew he'd had more than a few glimpses of her panties.

She should be embarrassed, but she couldn't muster the will. She'd never been very good at flirting before, but Tavis Neade brought out the temptress in her, and she intended to make full use of that side of her personality until she had all of him. Not just his mouth and tongue. She'd never been more certain she wanted his cock inside her too.

If it felt that good having the man's lips on her pussy, how much better would it be if he replaced his tongue with his erection?

She was trembling and a bit shaky as she made her way to the bathroom to splash water on her face. She needed a few minutes alone before she met him in the kitchen.

She stared at her face in the mirror first. She hardly recognized the woman staring back at her. Her hair was a mess. Her cheeks were red. And she was smiling as if she'd won the lottery.

After running a brush through her hair to tame it, she smoothed her hands down Tavis's shirt and lifted the front of it to inhale his scent. Powerful. Masculine. Delicious. She couldn't wait to press her nose against his neck, his chest, his cock. Scent him the way he'd done her. How long was he going to make her wait to have more of him?

CHAPTER 11

Turned out that answer was *indefinitely*.

Things changed between them. Tavis started holding her hand when he walked her to class. He also kissed her chastely on the lips and looked into her eyes and stroked her cheeks and let his gaze roam up and down her body at times throughout the day.

At night, he dropped onto his side of the bed, rolled toward her, pinned her under the covers, and made out with her as if they were randy teenagers.

By the end of their first month, four weeks after she'd met him, she was a constant ball of nervous energy. Sexual energy. It was hard to focus on her classes and her lab work. She went to the library between classes to do research but struggled to concentrate.

Tavis was always nearby. Always watching her. It was maddening.

On Friday, she didn't feel well. She went to class, but she ended up rushing to the bathroom and vomiting, lucky to have made it. She was shaky and flushed.

Tavis was standing outside the bathroom, hovering

when she came out. "You okay?" He grabbed her hand to stop her, keeping her from ducking and rushing past him.

"Yep," she lied. Who wanted to discuss their stomach issues with their boyfriend? Her masturbation habits, sure. Her vomiting, no.

"Did you drink any water by accident?" His brows were furrowed when he lifted her chin, forcing her to meet his gaze.

"I don't think so."

"Could be dysentery. Maybe from brushing your teeth or even the shower. Be careful not to swallow the water, okay?"

"Yes." Of course. She knew that. She'd done her homework before leaving the States. Besides, everyone knew not to consume water in any foreign country. It was never wise.

Saturday morning started much the same way. Her stomach was upset even before she got out of bed, and she slid off the side and nearly ran into the bathroom, not able to take the time to shut and lock the door.

Tavis was behind her in an instant, holding her hair back and stroking her head. He reached for a washcloth next and poured clean bottled water on it before wiping her face and then holding it against her forehead. "Maybe it's the flu," he suggested as he helped her back to bed. "Lie down. I'll make you some tea."

She watched as he left the room. The sun was barely up. She'd worked hard all week and intended to sleep a bit later than usual this morning before hitting the library for the rest of the day.

When Tavis returned with the steaming cup of tea, she pushed to sitting and sipped it.

"Better?" He looked far too concerned, his face tense, brows furrowed.

"I'm sure it's no big deal. Like you said, I probably ingested some water or maybe it's the flu." She drew her arms in close to her body, holding the mug in both hands, and then she winced. Her boobs were tender.

"What?" Tavis didn't miss a damn thing. He was more in tune with her than she was. *Shit, the man hasn't slept with me, but he probably knows my menstrual cycle.*

Wait… "Oh, shit." Her eyes widened and she nearly dropped the tea.

Luckily, Tavis took it from her trembling hands and set it on the bedside table.

No. No way. Fuck. "How long have we been here?" *Please, God. Maybe it hasn't been a month. Maybe it's only been a few weeks.*

"Four weeks. Why?"

Colette couldn't breathe. She jerked to the side and curled into a ball on the bed. She squeezed her eyes shut and tried to think. This couldn't be happening. Her fucking period. She hadn't had it since she arrived.

Her heart was pounding. *Oh, God.*

"Colette. What's going on?"

"Give me a minute," she managed to mumble.

"No." His hand was on her hip. "You're scaring me. Talk to me."

She tried to draw in a breath, unsuccessfully. Her head was spinning.

Tavis was crowding her. Taking up all the oxygen in the room.

She winced, needing him to leave.

"Colette?" he whispered.

"For the love of God, Tavis," she gritted out, not looking at him. "Give me a minute. Please. Get out."

He hesitated and then slid off the bed and left the room, shutting the door with a soft snick.

Colette drew in a deep breath, but couldn't release it.

Tears came to her eyes. This couldn't be happening. She was going to hyperventilate. She couldn't catch her breath. *No. God, no.*

Visions from that damn night of partying sprang to mind. Flashes of dancing with her friends, drinking too much, hooking up with a stranger.

Seriously, she didn't even know the guy's name. She knew nothing about him. She'd been drunk and feisty and wanted to blow off steam. It wasn't like her. She never hooked up with random men in bars. Strangers. *Never.*

Her stomach revolted again, and she shoved off the bed and ran to the bathroom, barely making it to the toilet this time before dry heaves shook her entire frame. This wasn't just morning sickness. It was also nerves. Fear. Panic.

She nearly jumped out of her skin when a hand landed on her back. She was slumped over the toilet seat, leaning all her weight on it, done vomiting but unwilling to move. She'd like to go ahead and drown herself for her stupidity.

"Sit back, hon." His voice was gentle, caring.

She didn't deserve it. She shook her head slightly, wincing as the nausea returned. Her punishment for being a reckless idiot.

Tavis ignored her protest and eased her away from the toilet.

She leaned against the wall and drew her knees up to her chest, wrapping her arms around them and facing the floor. She had his shirt pulled down over her knees. Tavis's shirt. Tavis. The man she'd been sharing a bed with for two weeks who was not the father of this baby.

More tears fell. She couldn't stop them.

Tavis squatted in front of her and wiped her face with a fresh clean washcloth.

"Stop being nice to me," she murmured, not looking at

him. She couldn't. She would start bawling if she did. Why was he still in here helping her? Was he dense? Surely he grasped what was happening.

He stepped over to the sink. The sound of a box opening filled her ears and then a wrapper. She held her breath and then glanced up as he held out a pregnancy stick. "Jesus," she murmured.

"I went to the pharmacy. Come on. Rip off the Band-Aid. We can't deal with the unknown."

She stared at his outstretched hand and the fucking pregnancy test for long seconds. Finally, she reached out and took it from him, trembling. More tears fell. "I think I'd rather be ignorant."

"No, you wouldn't. It will eat you up inside."

He was right. Why did he have to be so damn nice and right? And kind. And thoughtful.

She was half in love with him and now poof, their relationship was suddenly over before it began.

"I'll wait in the bedroom or I can stay here if you want."

She flinched. "Are you kidding?" Her hand was shaking and she didn't take her eyes off the fucking stick.

"No."

"You'd stay in here and hold my hand while I pee?" She couldn't even wrap her head around that idea.

"Yes." His tone was unreadable. He was stating facts. He didn't even know a thing about who'd gotten her pregnant or the circumstances, but he wasn't leaving her to deal with it alone.

A sob escaped.

He squatted down next to her again and lifted her chin, forcing her to meet his gaze for the first time since this shitshow had started. How long had it been? Minutes? An hour? Long enough for him to go to the pharmacy apparently.

"One thing at a time, okay? Right now, all you need to do is pee. That's it. Don't think about one other thing. Pee and then let me know when you're done."

She nodded.

He helped her stand on shaky legs. "Got it?"

"Yes." She felt like she was on autopilot. Pee on the stick. Just that one thing. That's all she needed to do for now.

As soon as Tavis pulled the door almost closed, she wiggled her panties down and sat on the toilet. She nearly dropped the damn stick in the toilet from shaking so badly. When she was done, she set the stick on the box it came in and washed her hands.

Before she turned off the water, Tavis was back. He guided her out of the room and back to her bed, lifting her up and settling her on the cool sheets. He even pulled the covers over her lower body.

She immediately rolled to her side, and Tavis shocked her yet again by climbing up behind her and spooning her. He stroked her hair back from her face. "Take a breath," he whispered.

"Why are you being so nice to me?"

"Because we're in a relationship, hon. I'm not an asshole."

She sobbed, more tears falling. Would they ever stop?

"It might be easier if you were an asshole," she murmured between sobs.

"Well, I'm not."

"You aren't even asking me questions. You should be furious."

"We'll get to the questions later. And why should I be furious?"

"Because I obviously had sex with someone else."

"I've had sex with other people too, hon. You haven't

had sex with anyone since I met you. Why would I be mad you slept with other people before we met?"

She choked on another sob, frustrated by his kindness. Part of her wished he would shout at her and fucking leave the room so she could torture herself in peace. Her life was ruined. Didn't he see that?

"Shh. Colette, you're going to make yourself sick. Deep breaths."

She jerked her face around to see him, glaring. "I fucking slept with another man the night before I met you, Tavis."

"Okay. And we'll deal with it. Together."

"Aren't you freaking out?" she shouted. Why was she angry with him?

"Yes. Of course I am, but not for the reasons you think."

"I'm pregnant with another man's baby, Tavis," she pointed out. She didn't need the stupid test to know. She was two weeks late. She was never late.

"Are you in love with him?" he asked, his face flat. He knew the answer.

"I don't even fucking know his name," she yelled before she could stop herself. She twisted away from him and buried her face in the pillow.

He held her a moment and then eased off the bed. "Be right back."

She held her breath while he was gone, not exhaling until he was back. He didn't say a word, just curled up behind her again.

Seconds ticked by. She knew by his silence there had been two lines on that stick. The infuriating man simply held her, stroking her cheek, smoothing her hair back. "I know you're freaking out, hon, but I'm here. I want to be here. We can lie here a while if you want. When you're ready to talk, let me know."

"What if I want you to leave the apartment so I can wallow in self-pity?"

"I won't do that. Sorry. My job is to protect you. I didn't like leaving you to go to the pharmacy. I only did it because I knew it was close. I jogged."

She drew in a slow breath. "What am I going to do?"

"I don't have the answers, but please let me in. Let me help."

She let out her breath and drew in another. The world felt like it was ending. Would she have to go home? Give up her dream? She was so close to finishing her PhD. *Fuck.*

"Are you certain who the father is?" he asked carefully.

"I'm certain I don't have a clue who the father is, if that's what you're asking. Not because I slept with more than one man. I only slept with the one man this year. One time. I was drunk. I was angry. I let him fuck me in his truck behind the bar. It was stupid. I'm an idiot. I'll obviously pay for it for the rest of my life."

"So, you didn't get his name. Do you remember anything else about him?" Tavis inquired.

"Sure. He was friendly, cute, flirty, about your size, sexy, dark hair, tanned skin."

"So, he looked like me," Tavis teased.

"It's not funny."

"It kinda is. I must be your type then."

"Ugh." She rolled her face into the pillow again.

"Sorry. I'm just trying to get you to relax a little."

"I'm not going to relax again for the rest of my life. It's a baby. That wasn't in the plan at all. I have another year of school. I didn't even have marriage on the horizon, let alone kids."

Tavis continued to stroke her. He'd moved to her arm now. "Did you want kids?"

"Sure. Maybe. In the future. Not now. Hell, I don't

know. I didn't really see myself falling for a man at all, so I hadn't factored in kids. They hadn't been on my radar. Not until..." She stopped speaking, biting her lip.

"I hope the rest of that sentence involved me," he murmured.

"Does it matter anymore?"

"Yes."

"Why? Why wouldn't you run as far as you can? Find someone to replace you before you get any more tangled with me and my stupidity."

"Not my style. Or if it was, it isn't anymore. Not since I met you. Does this put a crimp in our plans? A bit, yes, but you matter to me, so I'm not going to run out the door and leave you to deal with this alone."

"You barely know me."

"That's not true, and you know it. We've spent nearly every waking hour together for a month. Sleeping hours too. I know you better than any woman I've ever dated. I know you well enough to realize you're in a full panic right now and the last thing you need is for me to leave you alone."

Colette held her breath again, not wanting to cry anymore. Silent tears fell anyway.

"Did you have any feelings for this guy?"

"No. I didn't really talk to him. We fucked. We apparently didn't use protection."

"Any chance you could pick him out of a lineup?"

"I doubt it. My memory is fuzzy. I can't really visualize his face." She groaned. "Who the fuck sleeps with a man in his truck behind a bar with no protection?" She flattened her palm on her forehead.

"Lots of people."

"Have you?"

"Well, I don't think I've ever forgotten protection, but

I have had sex with women without getting their names a few times. Or maybe I got their names but then forgot. Not proud of it, but I've done it. Not much different from what you're describing. You're not the only person alive to have gotten drunk and had sex with a stranger, hon."

She chewed on her bottom lip. She knew he was trying to make her feel better, but she was fucking pregnant so it wasn't working.

"Do you want to try to find him?"

"No." She shook her head. "Definitely not."

"Okay, then one more question. Don't take this the wrong way. I'm just asking. Do you want to stay pregnant?"

She closed her eyes again and shuddered at the thought of the alternative. "I don't think I have it in me to terminate it."

"Okay. That's off the table then. So, you'll carry it to term. You don't have to make any decisions right now, but you could either keep it or arrange an adoption if you don't think you're ready to have a baby. See? Options?"

She twisted to face him again. He continued to shock her. "Not going to lie. Doubt I could give up a baby I carried inside me. It's part of me."

"Then you don't have to."

"Do you have an answer for everything?"

"No. Mostly I only have questions. I'm trying to be strong for you, Colette. I'm trying to be the kind of man you need right now."

"Is that hard?" She didn't know why she was pushing him. No reason to be a bitch.

"Not at all." He didn't flinch. Didn't take her question as a personal affront.

"So what? We're just going to go on as we have? You

still want to be with me now that I'm carrying another man's baby?"

Tavis drew in a long deep breath. "Like I said, I don't have all the answers. I'm not going to walk away from you though. I'm here. I'm not some random bodyguard. I'm your boyfriend. I know because you told Isaac," he teased as he gave her a squeeze.

"I'm also your friend. I care about you. This is a lot to process. All we can do is take it one day at a time."

"I don't deserve you."

"Of course you do. And I'm not going anywhere."

She twisted to look at him again. "You can't. My dad is paying you to stick to me like glue."

He lifted a brow. "You know good and well I could get another guy from the Holt Agency to take over for me. I could have done that at any point. I didn't because I don't want someone else protecting you, and I don't want to leave you. That hasn't changed."

"Surely you're freaking out inside."

"Yep." At least he didn't lie. He leaned closer. "But I was already freaking out inside before today. I've never had a serious girlfriend. I've never been remotely as close to anyone as I am to you."

"You've never had a relationship that lasted longer than a month?" She didn't believe that.

"I have. I've even had one that lasted almost a year, but I didn't spend as much time with her in that year as I have with you in one month. Nor did I ever see it as a long-term thing. I never felt my chest tighten when she entered a room. I never paced around waiting for her phone calls. I never thought long and hard about her when we weren't together. She was just a woman I was exclusive with for a year. We went our separate ways. Neither of us lost sleep when we broke up."

Colette could understand that. She shouldn't be judging him. She'd never been even remotely invested in another person before Tavis. And now…

She shuddered. There was no reason to ponder what was going to happen next. If he stayed with her through this, he was the best man alive. She didn't even feel like staying with *herself* at the moment.

"Why don't you take a shower," he suggested. "I'll make you something to eat."

She cringed at the thought of swallowing.

"Oatmeal or toast. You need something inside your stomach."

She stared at him. Was he real? She'd spent two weeks trying to get in his pants. Now what? He'd probably never want to have sex with her now. That ship sailed.

Tavis cupped her face though and gently kissed her. "One hour at a time today, okay?"

She nodded. What choice did she have?

CHAPTER 12

Colette pulled away from him over the next few days. She went through the motions of showering, dressing, eating—though not much—but she didn't meet his gaze, and she didn't come very close to him.

He knew she was hurting, processing, thinking, and he wanted to give her space, but it was hard to judge how much space he should give her and for how long.

Had he said the right things Saturday morning? He wasn't sure. He thought so.

He was processing too. This was huge. Monstrous. The woman he'd fallen hard for was pregnant with another man's baby. He didn't know how to feel about that but he tried not to think too hard.

Colette was the same woman he'd grown to care for. It was way too soon to toss around the L word, but his feelings for her ran deep and strong.

He needed to be careful. She was fragile. He could hurt her if he went full steam ahead and then couldn't take the heat. The crazy thing was that part of him knew there was nothing to consider. She was already his. There was no going back.

He had to ask himself, would he leave her if she were injured or sick or had cancer or lost a limb? No. Then why would he break up with her because she was pregnant?

She'd made it clear that she'd never had feelings for the man she'd had sex with, had no interest in finding him, and had no thoughts of terminating the pregnancy.

It was simple. He still felt the same about her.

But she'd pulled away from him, which he also understood. All he could do was give her space. She needed time.

Somehow she'd rallied. She'd gone to the library all day Sunday. Though he caught her staring into space seeing nothing a few times, she'd also worked. He'd seen her poring over books and taking notes.

Now it was Monday. She'd had to return to class, face humans. And so far, she'd done so without seeming to miss a beat. He knew better, but her peers didn't.

While she was in her lab, his phone buzzed, and he stepped away to take the call from Ajax. He hadn't spoken to Ajax or Ryker since the big revelation. It was none of their business of course, but he also didn't want to sound off.

"Hey," he answered as he settled on a bench several yards from the lab, keeping his gaze on the door the entire time.

"Got a minute?"

"Yep."

"We did some digging around in Secretary Loughlin's life and came up with very little. I don't think the man has even cheated on his wife, which is saying something these days. He doesn't appear to have any inappropriate relationships, not even peripheral ones with known philanderers."

"That's good. It's a dead end, but it's still good." Tavis wondered how Colette would feel about him snooping in her father's private life. He hated keeping things from her. It made him nervous. But she didn't need any added burden. Unless he had something substantial to update her about, he would keep his digging around to himself.

"Still nothing on Steve Lacoste?"

"Nothing. Man's in the wind. But I did find something else that may or may not be interesting. Have you heard of Richard Tillerman?"

"No." Tavis straightened his spine. The name didn't ring a bell.

"Apparently she went on a few dates with him months ago and blew him off, but he hasn't taken the hint."

"What do you mean?" Tavis drew in a slow breath. He didn't like the way the hairs on the back of his neck stood on end.

"Her phone records indicate he texts her."

"Still? You mean recently?"

"Yes. Last week twice."

Tavis swallowed. That made no sense. Why would she be getting messages from a guy she dated months ago? *Does she respond to them?*

Tavis refused to allow himself to mistrust her. That was absurd. She'd never given him any reason to doubt anything she'd told him, but why would she be in communication with someone and not tell him? Especially if that someone was harassing her while Tavis was in the middle of trying to ascertain who the fuck might have a reason to bother her.

Tavis ran a hand through his hair. "I'll talk to her."

"Okay. How are things otherwise?"

They suck. Turns out she's pregnant from a one-night stand the day before I met her and yet I want her just as badly as I did before I found that out. "Fine."

Ajax chuckled. "I've never once heard you use that ridiculous word. What's going on? Anything I should know about?"

"I'm sure you already got the lowdown from Ryker."

"Yes. But update me. How serious is this?"

Tavis didn't want to have this conversation. Not today. "We're taking it slow."

"That's…interesting. Slow as in you haven't slept with her slow?"

He sure as fuck wasn't answering that question. "Slow as in I have to keep her safe for five more months and I don't want anyone else to do the job slow. Careful."

"Okay. That's good. I guess. You sound off. Like I hit a nerve."

"Nope." He needed to shut the fuck up. No way was he discussing even one detail of this situation with Ryker or Ajax. Not until he had to. He had ideas percolating in his head, and he didn't want to back himself into a corner.

"All right. Well, I gotta go. Serena is calling my name from upstairs."

Tavis chuckled. "I bet."

"Later."

"Later." Tavis lowered the phone and rubbed his temples. *Who the fuck is Richard Tillerman?* Tavis didn't want to flat out ask her because he'd have to admit they'd dug into her phone records. He was going to have to get creative. It really bothered him that she was getting texts from a man she used to date and didn't think it was worth mentioning.

He didn't have enough time to figure out how to deal with the situation either because minutes later Colette came out of class, spotted him, and headed his direction.

As was her usual for the last forty-eight hours, she kept her head down, didn't make eye contact with him, and grumbled something unintelligible when she reached him.

The true smack in the face happened when he reached for her bag and she didn't fight him on it. She let him take it from her.

She was exhausted. He knew she wasn't sleeping well, partly from how difficult it was trying to hug the edge of the bed to avoid touching him during the night and keep herself completely covered at all times.

He hated this. Hated how strained their relationship was. Hated that she'd pulled away from him. Hated that he couldn't think of a good way to inquire about Richard Tillerman.

When they got back to the apartment, she dragged herself upstairs and sequestered herself in her room without a word.

Tavis reminded himself that it would be inconsiderate and downright insulting of him to get angry with her. He wasn't the one with an unwanted pregnancy. He wasn't the one vomiting every morning as a constant reminder. The last thing she needed was a confrontation from the man she was in a relationship with.

They were in a relationship, right? Lately, he felt like he was no different from any previous bodyguard she'd had. He assumed she'd treated the long line of them the way she'd been treating Tavis for the past two days. He couldn't even blame her for that. And he would not.

He'd been doing most of the cooking, which he didn't mind. She had a heavy schedule. His job was simply to stay close to her. He could cook. He'd done most of it since they arrived. She hadn't eaten much in the past forty-eight hours, but he still set it in front of her.

When dinner was ready, he headed upstairs and knocked softly on her door.

She didn't respond, so he slowly opened it.

She was lying on the bed, curled up on her side, staring at nothing, eyes red-rimmed, face splotchy. She'd been crying again.

He wasn't sure she even knew he'd knocked or entered. He approached slowly, hoping he wouldn't scare her to death. His chest was tight. He hated seeing her like this. The Colette he'd gotten to know for the past month—the temptress—was gone. In her place was a shell of a woman who was hurting.

He sat on the edge of the bed and set a hand on her hip. He'd hardly touched her lately, and she winced at the contact that wasn't even direct skin to skin.

"Want to talk?" he asked.

She shook her head.

"Will you come down and eat? You're not getting enough calories."

"Every time I eat, my stomach revolts."

"I've noticed, but you have to try. I made stir-fry. I kept all the parts separate. Maybe you could eat rice with nothing on it? Or plain chicken or vegetables?" He glanced at her frame. She'd lost weight already from not eating.

"You have health insurance through the university, right? Maybe you should make an appointment with the clinic to make sure you're doing everything you should be."

She closed her eyes. "I will. Soon."

"I bet I could at least get prenatal vitamins from the pharmacy if you'd like. They don't require prescriptions for them here."

She slowly turned to face him. "Stop being nice."

He sighed.

"Just...Tavis, I don't deserve nice right now. It's annoying."

"Hon, you haven't done anything wrong. Life threw you a curveball. You don't deserve to be punished for it."

She jerked to sitting, swatting his hand off her thigh. "I'm an idiot. I fucking had unprotected sex with a stranger. I need you to be mad about it. All this...nice...is too much. It's driving me crazy."

"Do you think I'm not mad?" His voice rose. He didn't want to lose his cool with her, but she was pushing him to at least defend himself. "I'm furious. You know why? Because this one tiny indiscretion has stolen my sweet, beautiful, innocent Colette from me. My temptress. I want her back. I want her to stop punishing herself for a momentary error in judgment and look at me the way she did up until Saturday morning. I want her to smile and joke around and flirt with me mercilessly."

"I can't."

"And I get that, and I'll give you all the time and space you need. But don't ask me not to be nice because I care about you and I'm hurting too because I miss you."

She hesitated, staring at him for a long time, and then she lurched forward and wrapped her arms around him, coming up on her knees to get closer.

Blessed angels.

"I'm sorry. I'm a fucking disaster."

He slid his hands up her back, grateful for the contact. Anything at this point would be appreciated. "I know, hon. Don't shut me out. Let me help. Yell at me if you need to. Talk to me. Whatever's going through your head needs an outlet. Don't hold it all in. You need someone to talk to, and that someone is me."

"It's hard," she whispered against his neck. "I spend half the day trying to pretend this nightmare isn't real. I keep wishing I would miscarry or something, and then I feel guilty. It's not this baby's fault I fucked up."

"You didn't fuck up, Colette." He hugged her tighter.

"There's a human being inside me. Growing. He or she deserves a good life. I'm a good person. I can do that. I might not be able to fulfill my previous dreams, but I can be a good mom."

Tavis leaned back a few inches and met her gaze. "You'll be the best mom, and you don't have to give up your dreams. You can have both."

She sighed. "Don't see how that's possible. I'm fooling myself by staying here and going through the motions of classes and labs. How the hell am I going to finish my last semester and work on my dissertation and all by next summer while also dealing with morning sickness, exhaustion, oh, and let's not forget the fact that this baby will be born in the middle of the fucking spring semester."

"You'll figure it out. I know you will. You have people. Your parents love you. And you have me," he offered, meaning it.

She groaned. "My parents? Are you kidding? They'll probably disown me. Every time I think about telling them, I get sick all over again. I'm living a lie, going to classes as if nothing is wrong. I don't want to tell them because if I do, they'll make me come home. They'd probably try to either hide me in the basement or send me to some sort of nineteen fifties facility for unwed girls as if I were a wayward teenager."

He chuckled. "You're kind of old for that, and I don't think they have places like that anymore."

"I bet they do," she argued. "Or worse…" she shuddered.

"If they knew right now, you know what they'd do? They'd tell me to go out with some guy I hate and have sex with him and then convince him the baby was his."

Tavis's eyes shot wide. "They would do that?"

"In a heartbeat."

"How would the guy buy it? It's not like you got pregnant yesterday."

"I'm sure they'd manage to convince him somehow."

Tavis drew in a deep breath. "So, don't tell them. Stay here. Keep working on your dream. After a while, it will be too late for any of that." He hated knowing her parents could be so highhanded with her. Even if they really shouldn't have any pull in her life—after all, she was a fucking grown woman—the fact that they would even try crawled up under his skin and made him furious.

She chewed on her bottom lip. "Have you told anyone?"

"Fuck, no," he retorted immediately. "Not anyone else's business."

She swallowed. "So, no one knows but you and me so far?"

"Unless you've told someone."

She shook her head. "Who the hell would I tell?"

"Don't you talk to your girlfriends?"

"What girlfriends?"

"I assume you must have a posse. Who did you go out with that night before you came here?" He knew she'd been with three women.

"Yeah. Those were friends from undergrad. I see them now and then. We don't have enough in common for more than that. Plus, the only way to go out with them is if I sneak out like I did that night. Like I'm fucking fifteen."

He furrowed his brow. "Have you always lived at home?"

She shook her head. "No. Rarely since I left for college. Holidays and some summers. I've usually lived in an apartment, but my father hates it. Thinks it's not safe. Hires people to fucking guard me even when I'm home. Leaving my own apartment to go out is the same as sneaking."

He chuckled, picturing her super-sleuth skills trying to get away from her overbearing parents. She was twenty-seven, for fuck's sake.

"I'm sorry," he murmured, more convinced than ever to make sure this study abroad went perfectly for her without a hitch. No wonder she wanted to come to Africa to do a semester of research. It was as far away from her controlling parents as she could get. No wonder she also didn't want them to know a thing about her life.

Her voice was soft and nervous when she spoke again. "You seriously won't tell anyone? Not your bosses or my father?"

"Not a chance. They didn't hire me to snitch. They hired me to protect you. And I'll keep doing that for as long as you let me."

She leaned into him again. "Thank you. I'm not sure what it will change since I'll obviously have to return to the States six months pregnant, but at least no one will be able to hide it or deny it or force me to do anything I don't want to do."

"I'll do everything in my power to ensure you have these next five months of peace, Colette. At some point, you'll have to start wearing looser clothes just in case someone snaps a picture, but we can do this."

She smiled. There was a God. "Thank you. This is the first moment in three days I've felt like I have at least half a plan that doesn't make me want to vomit."

He slid a hand up to her face and stroked her hair back. "You've got this. I'm here for you." He leaned in slowly and was relieved when she let him kiss her lips. He kept it chaste, but it was something. "Now, please come downstairs and eat."

CHAPTER 13

The next morning, Colette's phone rang incredibly early. Long before the alarm went off.

Colette moaned in confusion, so Tavis sat up, reached across her, and snagged it from her bedside table, glancing at the screen to see who was calling. "It's your father," he murmured.

She groaned as she took it from him. "I better answer or he'll just keep calling until I do."

Tavis nodded and dropped onto his side next to her. He didn't really want to climb out of bed, and he doubted she had anything to say that would be so private she wouldn't want him to hear.

Colette connected the call. "Dad? Why are you calling so early?"

The man's voice was so loud, Tavis could hear every word. "Oh. I didn't realize how early it was. I wanted to catch you before you got too busy to answer. You haven't called home in weeks."

"That's because I'm busy."

"Doing what?" The man sounded genuinely perplexed.

Tavis's brows shot to his hairline. *What the fuck?* He watched Colette grit her teeth and roll her eyes before she schooled her voice to respond with a deep breath. "I'm working on my PhD, Dad. I'm not on vacation."

"Of course. No reason to get snippy. Surely you have time to call home."

Tavis wasn't sure why she would ever call home if this was how her father spoke to her. No wonder she had a strained relationship with the man.

"Listen, I spoke to Richard Tillerman the other day. He came to my office."

Tavis's hackles rose, and he watched as Colette pursed her lips and held her breath. She looked like her head might explode. She didn't respond. Tavis doubted she could without screaming. Tavis was even more curious to know about Richard Tillerman and his story. Plus, he had a reason to ask now.

William Loughlin continued, "He said he's been texting you and you never respond."

"Why on earth would he tell you that?" she snapped.

"Don't use that tone with me, Colette. He simply asked if you had a new number. What I want to know is why you aren't answering him. He's a nice man. Perfect for you. Lord knows anyone who would continue to pursue you when you ignore them is someone worth paying attention to."

"Stay out of it, Dad," she gritted out. Her knuckles were white. If she could, she would have made the phone buckle in half. Tavis could feel the rage wafting off her. "It's none of your business. I'll choose who I date and don't date, and I'm not dating Richard Tillerman. Case closed."

"Why not? Give me one good reason? He's good looking, hardworking, and intelligent. His family is influential and wealthy. He's the perfect match for you."

"Not going to happen. Don't ask again."

"Colette," the man barked. "You're being unreasonable."

She sat upright. "No, Dad. *You're* being unreasonable. If you like the man so much, you go out with him. Do not call me at the crack of dawn to fix me up with men, Dad. I'm not even on the same continent as Richard. Goodbye." She ended the call, her hands shaking.

For a moment, Tavis thought she might launch it across the room, and he wouldn't blame her. He might grab it and do so himself.

Finally, with a growl of frustration, she tossed it onto the mattress and bolted from the bed, running for the bathroom.

He was used to her stomach being unsettled in the morning. It had been every day so far, but he hated that she had more than one reason to vomit today. Tavis swung his legs over the edge of his side of the bed and rushed after her, catching up and grabbing her hair just in the nick of time before she started heaving into the toilet.

At least now Tavis knew why there were incoming texts from Richard Tillerman. And he had a reason to inquire. Though it was painfully obvious *why* the man was texting, Tavis didn't understand why Colette hadn't mentioned a word?

Granted, Colette was entitled to some privacy, but Tavis had specifically asked her if she knew anyone who could be a threat for any reason. She should have mentioned Tillerman. The man was phone stalking her. And he'd gone to her father's office? What the fuck?

When Colette finished dry heaving, Tavis handed her a cold damp cloth. This was their daily routine. In a moment she would drop onto her butt and groan before telling him she didn't like him following her into the bathroom to watch her heave.

Today was different though. She did drop onto her butt and lean against the wall to wipe her forehead and then her lips, but she didn't speak. Instead, she stared at the floor.

"Sorry about that," she finally whispered.

Tavis winced. "Sorry about what? You didn't do anything."

She shrugged. "You didn't need a firsthand, front-seat spot for the William Loughlin sideshow."

He chuckled and squatted down next to her. "I didn't mind. It helps me understand you better."

"I'm sure you didn't want to know any of that. It's embarrassing."

He cleared his throat and went straight for the elephant. "Why didn't you tell me about Tillerman?"

"That's also embarrassing."

"Why?" He was beyond confused. If a man Colette had dated even one time was harassing her, he was a suspect, and Tavis needed to know about it. This made no sense.

"It just is. Please drop it. I don't want to discuss Richard."

Tavis stiffened. Something was off. "How long ago did you date him?" He tried not to let his voice sound accusatory, but was pretty sure he failed.

She jerked her gaze up and glared at him. "Several months, and I never once let the man touch me." She shuddered from head to toe, her face scrunching up in disgust. "So don't fucking look at me like that. He's not the father of the baby. I didn't lie to you. I haven't had sex with anyone for over six months. And I've *never ever* had sex with Richard. The paternity is not in question."

"Okay," he said softly. "I didn't mean to…"

"Yes, you did." She dropped her face. Her voice was steady and filled with defeat. "And you have every right. I get it. How the fuck could you possibly trust me?"

Tavis reached forward and lifted her chin, his chest tightening. "That's not true. I do trust you. I'm sorry for my momentary lack of sanity. If I'd thought it through for half a second, I would have realized how stupid my train of thought was. Please, forgive me."

She nodded and dropped her face again the moment he released her chin.

Tavis waited a few moments and then spoke again, trying to keep his voice calm. "If someone is harassing you, Colette, no matter how minor it may seem, I need to know about it. I can't protect you if I don't have all the information."

She inhaled slowly and spoke to the floor. "It's no big deal. He's just persistent. Please drop it."

"It's obviously a big deal or you wouldn't react so viscerally to the mention of his name. I can dig around and find out anything I want to know about Richard Tillerman, Colette, but I'd rather hear most of it from you."

She shoved off the floor and scrambled to her feet, stomping into the bedroom where she climbed back into bed. It was still super early. The sun wasn't even up.

Tavis left the light on in the bathroom when he joined her, the fine hairs on the back of his neck standing on end. He sat on the edge of the bed and waited.

After a few minutes of silence, she spoke, not looking at him. "He's the son of one of my father's friends. A banker, same as his father. Masters in business or some shit. He doesn't give a shit about me. He only cares about the connections he thinks I could provide if he married the secretary of state's daughter."

Tavis flinched. *Married?* "Has he asked you to marry him?"

She sighed and whispered, "Yes. Flippantly. More like

pointed out the benefits. As if it were a business negotiation one might have on a first date."

Tavis sat up straighter. "And you don't think that's important?" Part of him wanted to shake her, but he sensed she was withholding some piece of information. Maybe protecting Richard? Why would she do that?

"It's not." She groaned and rolled onto her back. "Tavis, I'm begging you to drop it."

He stared at her. She wasn't telling him something. He was sure of it, but now wasn't a good time to pressure her. She was exhausted and hungry and undoubtedly had an upset stomach. "Okay," he said softly as he lifted one of her hands and rubbed his cheek with it. "For now."

"Thank you."

"Want to get in the shower? I'll go make you some toast and bring it up."

"Thank you for that too." She smiled, but it was forced.

The irony in all this was that she had gotten extremely defensive thinking he didn't trust her, and yet, she was absolutely intentionally withholding information.

As soon as Tavis reached the kitchen, he lifted his phone and shot off a quick email to Ajax and Ryker. He wanted to know every damn detail about Richard Tillerman. He didn't even feel guilty about it. Colette had to know the first thing Tavis would do would be to dig around in the man's history.

Which meant whatever was going on or had gone on between Colette and Tillerman wasn't something Tavis would easily uncover on his own. Something personal had happened between them. But what? And what could be so embarrassing that Colette would seal her lips about it? She hadn't even had sex with the man. What else was there?

CHAPTER 14

Things between Tavis and Colette didn't improve much over the next two weeks. Colette kept him at arm's length. She didn't completely ignore him anymore, but she didn't share much either. She was polite and cordial, but withdrawn and quiet.

He gave her the space. He didn't have a choice. It hurt. He wanted to hold her. He wanted her to talk to him. But he wouldn't force her, and he couldn't begin to know what might have been going on in her mind.

A brief conversation a week ago had led to Colette agreeing to spend her fall break on the other side of the country doing a safari and tracking gorillas in the impenetrable forest.

Tavis made all the arrangements and felt like a weight lifted when they woke up Saturday morning and headed to the small airstrip where they would take a six-seater to the western side of Uganda.

Colette had been gradually improving in the mornings. She hadn't been violently sick in several days. He assumed their new routine had something to do with her easing queasiness.

Every morning, Tavis got up before her, made her a cup of herbal tea and plain toast. She carefully sat upright in bed and slowly ate the toast and drank the tea. It was working, so he kept doing it.

When they reached the airport, Colette grabbed his hand to stop him.

He turned toward her, concerned.

She tipped her head back and smiled up at him. "Thank you."

"For what, hon?"

"For planning all this. For distracting me. For cooking and cleaning and making sure I get enough to eat. I mean it. I appreciate everything you've done. I know it hasn't been easy. I've been a bitch. Moody. Angry. Unreachable."

He threaded their fingers together and lifted their combined hands to his lips, kissing her knuckles. "I know everything about our relationship is odd and awkward right now, but my feelings for you haven't changed. I care deeply about you. I've been trying to give you space to work through the cacophony of noise in your head. I hope you can relax for a week, let yourself go into vacation mode. Forget the rest of the world exists and just enjoy yourself."

She smiled, the first genuine smile he'd seen in weeks. It warmed his heart. "I can do that."

"Good."

Thirty minutes later, she was grinning even wider as the plane rose to six thousand feet and settled at that height.

Tavis sat next to her behind the pilot, threading their fingers together. His face hurt from smiling back at her. She was lighter, excited, enjoying herself.

Her expression was bright as she pointed out the gorgeous countryside below them. She shouted when she wanted to speak to be marginally heard through their headsets. He could read her lips well enough though as she pointed out Lake Victoria and then the many dirt roads that most of the country was covered with.

The hills were gorgeous, covered with coffee and bananas and tea. Everything was lush and green. The country had the perfect environment for year-round crops. It may have been poor, but he'd come to learn that most of the inhabitants didn't know they were poor. They were living their lives. They had plenty to eat and all the clay right under their feet to make bricks and build one-room dwellings.

People in Uganda didn't spend much time inside. They worked the fields during the day and sat outside when they weren't working. The weather was phenomenal nearly all the time, the temperature warm but often mild. The shelter served one primary purpose—to protect the inhabitants from the rain and provide them with a safe place to sleep.

"My God," Colette mouthed as they swooped down low over the dirt runway. She pointed at the giraffes as they scattered in every direction. The pilot had warned them they would probably do a drive-by to clear the runway of animals before landing on the second pass.

The giraffes were so majestic. Gorgeous creatures who took his breath away as they galloped on their long legs out of harm's way.

Finally, the plane landed. Colette's entire personality had undergone a transformation. She was giggling with glee as they climbed out of the plane and met their guide for the week.

"Tavis and Colette? I'm Marcus. I'll be your driver and tour guide for the week." Marcus shook their hands and nodded toward the Land Cruiser as he grabbed Colette's suitcase from the pilot.

Tavis grabbed his own bag, and moments later, their luggage was stowed in the back of the SUV and they were off.

Colette tipped her head back and smiled, window down, sun and wind hitting her face. "It's so beautiful here."

Tavis agreed, though he had trouble taking his eyes off the woman next to him.

"It's about an hour drive to Ishasha Lodge and then you can relax and enjoy the rest of your afternoon. I think you'll love the lodge. The food is amazing. It's located on the Ntungwe River. You can sit by the water and rest. We'll head out for our first safari drive in the morning."

"Sounds good," Tavis responded. All that mattered to him was seeing Colette relaxed and pleased. He wasn't stupid enough to think her problems were completely gone and ignored. She would carry the weight of her issues in the back of her mind during the entire vacation, but hopefully she could keep the future where it belonged and enjoy the moment.

After Marcus entered the national park, he put the Land Cruiser in park and turned in his seat. "Tavis, if you'll help me lift the roof, the two of you can climb up from the back seat and sit on the ledge behind the raised section."

Tavis was surprised and excited as he lifted the back while Marcus lifted the front.

Marcus pointed at the back row of seats. "Grab those pillows to sit on and climb on up."

Tavis wasn't sure if Colette would be game for this or not, but when he glanced at her, she was grinning from ear to ear as she made her way toward him. He steadied her around the waist to help her climb up and then followed to sit next to her.

When he turned to face her, she looked so happy. Content. Eyes wide as she looked around. "My God, it's so beautiful," she murmured as she reached for Tavis's hand and squeezed.

"Ready?" Marcus asked.

"Yep," Tavis responded.

And they were off. It took another half an hour to get to the lodge, during which they saw a lot of amazing animals ranging from buffalo to topi. Birds too. So many species of birds.

The lodge was breathtaking. Mostly outdoors with a dining area and seating next to the river. After dropping their bags off at the amazing cabin they would be staying in for the first few nights, they returned to the lodge to eat dinner and lounge next to the river on Adirondack chairs.

Colette sighed as she turned to meet Tavis's gaze. "What?"

"You look so happy," Tavis pointed out.

She leaned her head back and closed her eyes. "I am. At least for the next week I can pretend I'm someone else and ignore my problems."

He reached for her hand and brought it to his cheek. "You don't have to pretend to be someone else. The real you is amazing."

"The real me is pregnant and alone without finishing school."

He swallowed. "You're not alone, Colette," he whispered. God, he wished she could understand how much he cared about her. She was holding him at arm's length, and though he hated it, he wouldn't pressure her to see that she had him. She wasn't ready to deal with whatever the two of them could become. Tavis wasn't sure he was either.

In his heart, he was head over heels for this woman. But the reality was she was way out of his league, and even if she did decide to give him a shot at more after six months, how was he going to fit into her world?

Tavis had never been around rich people. Nor did he have any experience with government officials. He was certain her father would never approve of him, but he wasn't sure he gave a fuck. All that mattered was Colette.

He certainly didn't want to be the cause of a family rift or add to her pile of problems, but fuck. It was possible that even without her parents' approval of him, she would still be better off with him than holding on to whatever odd relationship she had with them.

If he walked away from her, what would happen to her? Would she move in with her parents and let them help her? Would they even let her move in? Would they even offer to help at all?

His stomach roiled every time he considered what she might face. She certainly knew better than he did, but she wasn't eager to talk about it, and he couldn't blame her. Nor was he eager to bring it up. There was plenty of time.

All Tavis wanted to do for the time being was lighten her load and make her smile, convince her she was his even though she was pregnant. With each passing day, he grew more and more certain he didn't give a fuck she was pregnant. It changed nothing about how he felt. It was more complicated, but when he thought about turning his back on her, he felt sick.

Hell, when he thought about not seeing her every single day, he felt sick. The idea of not waking up next to her— even with a seemingly giant valley between them—made his chest hurt.

He hadn't even had sex with her. Ever since those two lines had shown up on the stick, she'd pulled back and gone cold. Until today. Tonight, he was holding her hand. She was letting him. She was also smiling.

One of the park employees walked them to their cabin in the dark. Apparently there was a local hippopotamus that shared this area of the national park and sometimes wandered too close.

"Someone will set up hot water for you in fifteen minutes," their guide informed them. "So you can shower before bed."

"Thank you." Tavis shut the door and turned to find Colette wandering around the fancy glamping arrangement.

"This is the cutest place I've ever been," she said, twisting her neck back to look at the canvas ceiling. It was really a cross between a tent and a cabin. She giggled, which warmed his heart. "It cracks me up that they have to put a bucket of hot water outside so we can shower."

He smiled and reached for her, hoping she would come into his embrace and let the distance between them dissipate. He didn't fully breathe until she let him wrap his arms around her, and he gave a silent fist pump when she tipped her head back and let him kiss her.

He took his time, relearning what it felt like to lick the seam of her lips and swallow her soft sighs. He flattened his palm on the small of her back, his other hand reaching up to thread in her hair, angling her head to one side so he could slide his tongue into her mouth.

Yes. God, yes. He loved the way she softened for him, let him in. It was a small thing but a step in the right direction. Should he be doing this? Probably not. But fuck it. Pretending she wasn't his was ridiculous. He should be focused on convincing her of that fact, not trying to stay away from her.

He hated releasing her, but they needed to shower while the water was hot, so he eased back to stare into her eyes. "I could kiss you all night, but you should get in the shower."

"Yeah." She glanced away with a shiver, breaking the spell as she released him. She didn't meet his gaze as she grabbed her toiletries and headed for the attached bathroom. It wasn't really separate. It didn't have a door, but if he sat on the bed, he wouldn't be able to see her in the shower.

Lord knew he'd rather watch her shower or join her, but they weren't there yet. He wasn't sure when they might get there since she would undoubtedly grow self-conscious about her body soon. He hated that as much as he hated all the other parts of this situation that never leaned in his favor.

Colette was fucking gorgeous. She would be just as stunning if not more so pregnant. He'd never had thoughts of pregnancy or kids before. He'd never visualized having children with anyone he'd dated or seeing their body change and grow as the baby did. This was new to him. Shocking. Because it was Colette. Because he would take her any way he could.

When Colette returned, a towel wrapped around her, her fingers gripping it above her breasts as if the world might end if he saw more of her skin, he drew in a long slow breath and said nothing. He didn't remind her he'd already seen her naked. He did, however, come to her, lift her chin, and give her a chaste kiss to remind her who he was to her before he headed for the bathroom to shower.

It wasn't late, but it was dark and quiet, and there wasn't much else to do in the middle of the national park at night. They couldn't even leave the cabin without calling for an escort. So when Tavis returned to the bedroom to find Colette already under the covers, he turned off the lights and climbed in on the other side of her.

He didn't drop onto the top of the blankets. For the first time in their odd relationship, he crawled into the bed like a normal person and reached for her.

She gave a soft gasp as he pulled her into his arms, arranging her so she was snuggled against his chest, her head in the crook of his arm.

He wrapped his arm around her as her palm landed on his chest. This was better. She belonged in his arms. She didn't protest, though her breathing was heavier and she wasn't exactly relaxed. She was slightly stiff.

Tavis kissed the top of her head.

"Tavis…"

"I'm kinda done letting you have three feet of space in the bed, hon. I won't pressure you for more, though it is ironic how the tables have turned. But it's maddening being so close and yet so far. Please let me hold you."

"Okay," she whispered.

Thank God.

For the first time in weeks, Tavis actually fell asleep quickly and stayed that way.

CHAPTER 15

The next several days were like a dream. Colette forced her problems to the back of her mind and focused on the zebras, giraffes, buffalo, hippos, kob, and topi. They were even lucky enough to see a herd of elephants in the distance. There was no way she could ever describe what it was like to see African animals in the wild.

On top of that, Tavis was amazing. Almost to the point of being annoying. The man could do no wrong. He refused to be daunted by her situation. Any space he'd given her for the past two weeks disappeared.

She hadn't been certain where his head was in the weeks following the discovery that she was pregnant. He'd said all the right things when he'd spoken, but he'd kept his words to a minimum and touched her infrequently.

Had he done that for her or for himself? She didn't want to ask. It didn't matter. Either he'd given her time to think and adjust her mindset, or he'd taken his own time to come to grips with the fact that she was fucking pregnant with a baby that was not his.

Apparently, he was either done thinking or done giving her a wide berth because from the moment they'd begun this safari, he'd kept her close. Holding her hand had become the norm whenever they were walking. When they perched on the top of the Land Cruiser, he kept one hand on the small of her back protectively. And when they slept, he pulled her into his arms and never let her go.

Nights were her favorite, even though she felt like she was living a lie. Like her life was split in two. On Earth One, she was a single pregnant woman who hadn't finished her education and would soon find herself raising a child on her own while working and shuffling back and forth to daycare.

On Earth Two, she was a wealthy, carefree graduate student on the vacation of a lifetime with her boyfriend. She liked Earth Two better, but it wasn't real. It was fiction, and the bubble would eventually burst. It had no choice.

Letting Tavis get physically close to her wasn't hard. Her body hadn't changed much yet. Her breasts were usually tender and sore, but she didn't feel self-conscious about her stomach.

It was a slippery slope though. How was she going to break this contact when her pregnancy grew more obvious? She would feel uncomfortable about him touching her so much when she started growing. Wouldn't he?

The only things that stood out about this fake world was that neither of them ordered alcohol and she was so damn tired that she slept much more than she used to. Tavis didn't say a word about either. He didn't once order himself a beer or mention it, and he frequently was the one to suggest they go to bed earlier than usual.

After spending two nights at the first lodge and two

nights at yet another beautiful lodge in another park, they arrived at Bwindi Impenetrable Forest where they would go gorilla tracking the next day. This would be the highlight of the trip, and she was looking forward to it.

It seemed like every place they stayed was even better than the last. The Buhoma Lodge had quaint log cabins with deep clawfoot tubs. She spent a half an hour soaking on the first night.

It wasn't until she climbed into bed, giving up the bathroom to Tavis, that she opened her phone for the first time that day.

She cringed when she saw there were messages from Richard. Jesus. Why couldn't the man leave her alone? Her panic about what he might know about her was growing with every contact.

Even though she hadn't responded to his texts or his emails, she was on edge, wondering what he might do with the information he might have. She chewed on her fingernail as she read his text.

I know you're on the other side of the globe, but surely you can return my message, Colette. I'm trying to give you time to do the right thing, but I'm running out of patience.

Her stomach seized. What did he mean? She'd half-expected for his texts to take on this new tone for weeks. She shouldn't be surprised. But she'd hoped he wouldn't turn out to be as big of a dick as she suspected. Apparently, she'd been wrong.

After reading the text three times, hoping to hear a different tone or meaning, bile rose in her throat, and she dropped her phone and dashed for the bathroom without even thinking about the fact that Tavis was in the shower.

He was standing under the water, a half wall keeping

her from seeing below his waist, and she hesitated, slightly mortified for a moment, before rushing the rest of the way to the toilet and emptying her stomach of dinner.

"I'm so sorry," she murmured as she finally caught her breath, still leaning over the toilet. "I couldn't…"

Tavis's hand landed on her shoulder, and he pressed a cold washcloth against her forehead. "Don't apologize. Are you okay?"

She sighed. She wasn't. Not even close. This had nothing to do with morning sickness. This was all about Richard. She'd gone from pissed to nervous to scared now. And the last thing she wanted to do was tell Tavis what the fuck she was concerned about.

He helped her to her feet, and her breath caught in her lungs as her gaze landed on his chest. He was still dripping wet from the shower. The only thing he'd done was wrap a towel around his waist. At least she wasn't staring at his cock.

He brushed her hair back, tipped her chin, and met her gaze with a furrowed brow. "You haven't thrown up in the evening before, hon."

She shrugged. "I guess it can happen."

He nodded slowly. "I know it can, but are you sure it's not something else? Something you ate?"

She shook her head, not wanting him to think the food had been bad or uncooked or anything. Dinner had been perfect up until she'd seen the text from Richard.

He spun her around and led her back toward the bedroom, helping her to her side of the bed and pulling back the covers.

She gasped as her phone, which had been sitting on top, slid to his side, and then nearly died when the screen lit up. Shit. The last thing she wanted was for Tavis to see the texts from Richard. She prayed whatever was incoming was from anyone under the sun except for that fucking asshole. Even her dad. Anyone.

As Tavis reached for the phone, she held her breath, but her heart seemed to stop beating when he stiffened, holding the phone up.

"Oh, God," she whispered. Worse than another text. Richard had sent a photo this time. No words, just a picture of her on the dance floor with her friends the night before she'd flown to Uganda.

She somehow found the strength to snatch the phone out of Tavis's hand, but she was shaking and nearly dropped it.

Tavis took the cell back from her and patted the mattress. "Get in," he commanded.

She was shivering as she climbed under the covers. She wished she could slap her cell out of his hand, but didn't dare. Whatever was going to happen next on this train wreck was already in motion.

"When was this taken?" Tavis asked calmly. There was no accusation in his voice.

She dropped her head onto the pillow and stared at the ceiling. She was fucking scared now. Furious too. But mostly scared.

"Colette?" His voice was calm as he sat next to her hip and set his hand on her arm, giving it a squeeze. "I need you to talk to me, hon. What's going on?"

She inhaled slowly, mostly to keep from freaking the fuck out, and let that breath out just as slowly and deliberately. "I'm not sure."

Tavis lifted the phone to look at it again. "This is from the night before you left, isn't it?"

She closed her eyes and nodded. Tavis didn't know the

whole story. He couldn't possibly understand the scope of what was happening here. She wasn't sure *she* could fully wrap her head around it. She'd worried Richard's escalating texts might be leading up to something, but she hadn't thought about it being this.

"These texts are from Richard Tillerman, the man your father called you about. Was this asshole following you that night?"

"I don't know. Maybe," she murmured. "Or maybe he accidentally ran into me," she hedged, though she didn't believe that. Not deep down.

"You left out that detail when you told me about that night," he pointed out.

She winced.

Tavis slid his palm up to her neck. "May I please read what he has been texting you?"

Her heart was racing. She wasn't sure what to do. If she let Tavis read the texts, everything would change. He would know things she wasn't willing to face. He would ask hard questions she didn't want to answer.

Without answering him, she rolled away from him and curled into a ball. How did her life get so out of control?

Tavis set her phone down on the bedside table instead of poking around in it. He didn't say a word as he stood and returned to the bathroom.

Panic set in as she listened to the water running, the sound of him brushing his teeth, the toilet flushing. Him walking away without pressuring her further was almost worse.

When he reemerged, he turned out all the lights and climbed into bed, not touching her. For the past several nights, he'd pulled her into his embrace every night. Now there was suddenly a foot and two thousand miles between them.

Silent tears ran down her face. She'd been so emotional lately, and it was hard to know what to attribute her rollercoaster of feelings to. The pregnancy hormones ranked high on the list of culprits, but this situation with Richard could possibly break her.

Why couldn't she just tell Tavis everything?

Because you're embarrassed and humiliated.

Plus, she knew if she told him all the details, he would have his people hunt Richard down and that would make everything worse. Tavis might be amazing at finding people and digging around in their lives, but he didn't understand the world of politics and how easily someone's life could be completely ruined with one false move.

One false move caught on camera.

How many pictures did Richard have? Was he taunting her with this one? Letting her know there were others and if she didn't do what he wanted, he would show the world?

With every new text, her fears escalated. It was time to admit Richard Tillerman was blackmailing her. And it wasn't just her reputation he could take down. He could ruin her father.

No. Telling Tavis would be a disaster. She needed to do something though. She needed to respond to the text. Make Richard think she was considering his proposal. It would buy her some time. Hell, perhaps if she let him believe she was at least interested in talking when she returned home, maybe she could get him to see reason when he finally saw her. Hugely pregnant.

Maybe he would give up his pursuit when he found out. Why bother to ruin her or her father if he was no longer interested in the end goal? Because she knew all he cared about was a business merger that would elevate his status in society. Colette was nothing to him but arm candy in the form of the secretary of state's daughter. A catch.

She shuddered at the thought of ever letting that man touch her, let alone kiss her. The thought of having sex with him was abhorrent. But it would never come to that because he would give up his quest once he saw her.

Yes. That was the best plan. String him along. Convince him she was on board with the idea of marrying him. Put an end to what she now knew were silent threats.

Tavis rolled onto his side, facing away from her. It tore a hole in her heart. She was hurting him. Blocking him out. He had every right to be angry with her. But he didn't understand what she was dealing with. He couldn't. He didn't live in her world. He had no idea how many people in her position were practically forced to marry someone they didn't even like just to keep up appearances. It happened all the time.

Colette had feared something like this would happen for years. Not necessarily that she would end up the victim of blackmail, but something similar that would cause her to feel trapped into marriage.

It was her own fault. She never should have gone out that night. She never should have fucked a stranger in his fucking truck. For the millionth time, she was once again furious with herself for that impulsive act that stemmed from misdirected anger.

She would pay for her mistake for the rest of her life. Hopefully not by marrying Richard though. She had to hope she could text him just enough to string him along and then find a way to ensure he was one of the first people she saw when she returned to the States at the end of the semester.

He would take one look at her, and give up the fight. And why bother to resort to his plan to blackmail her when he realized marrying her would be an embarrassment?

It could work.

Colette would still pay. She would probably never finish her PhD. She could probably get a decent job with the amount of education and knowledge she had but nothing like what she'd planned.

Staying in Uganda for the rest of the semester was a joke. For what? Was she really going to spend her time buried in the library working on a dissertation she most likely couldn't finish?

Even under the best of circumstances, it would be nearly impossible to finish her research while breastfeeding and changing diapers with little to no sleep.

She stared at Tavis's broad shoulders. He wasn't sleeping. She could tell by his breathing. He was too still. How angry was he? She'd never seen him lose his temper. She deserved it. She deserved for him to flip to his other side and lay into her.

Part of her wished he would. She wouldn't feel quite as sick to her stomach if he would stop being so nice. She couldn't imagine going to sleep with this giant rift between them. It probably wasn't even possible. Her heart was racing and her chest was tight.

Tavis was the first man she'd ever really cared about. If she was completely honest with herself—which she didn't have the luxury of being—she would have to admit her feelings were far deeper than caring for him.

He made her laugh. He made her smile. He cooked for her and cleaned up after her. He held her hair when she vomited, even though it had to infuriate him to see her sick from the baby she was carrying that belonged to another man.

He didn't waver though. He'd given her space and time, but he hadn't fully pulled away until right now. He was solid and strong—emotionally and physically. He was a dream. A pipe dream.

She squeezed her eyes tight and pictured him in her life. What if she returned to the States as his girlfriend? Pregnant or not, her parents would freak the fuck out. She didn't much care what they thought, but Tavis might. He couldn't possibly understand how furious her father would be if she hooked up with such a common man.

The funny thing was Tavis was anything but common. The man was a retired Navy SEAL, for fuck's sake. He had a lot of training and education. He was knowledgeable about a wide range of subjects, including every inch of this beautiful country.

Tavis had planned this trip down to the minute details, leaving out nothing, ensuring the two of them had the time of their lives. And she had been enjoying every single moment until the fucking text and then picture from Richard.

There was no way Tavis would agree to her plan to string Richard along. It wouldn't even be fair to ask him and also pretend to be his girlfriend. Flames would come out of his head if he found out she was secretly flirting with Richard on the side even if it was all fake.

The entire situation was a shitshow, and she couldn't see any way out. Tears fell again. Fucking tears. She held her breath, willing them to stop. They dripped onto her pillow, and she didn't dare move an inch to swipe at them because she wouldn't risk Tavis knowing she was crying.

She thought she did a good job holding back the sobs that wanted to escape, but apparently not.

Tavis rolled onto his back, reached for her, and hauled her against his side into the position he'd held her every night lately.

A sudden sob slipped from her lips at his kindness.

He pulled her tighter against his chest and kissed the top of her head before dragging the corner of the sheet to wipe her cheeks.

That only made things worse. She was treating him horribly, and he was treating her like a princess in return.

She grabbed onto the edge of the sheet, pressed it against her face and cried. Really cried. Hard. Ugly cried. Unable to stop. She'd needed to let herself release all these emotions for days, weeks. Once the dam opened, there was no stopping the flow of water until it was drained.

Tavis held her the entire time, stroking her arm, kissing her temple and her forehead, rocking her gently in his arms. Being perfect, which made her cry longer.

Finally, she was worn out and done. She sniffled the last of the tears and curled into him. "I'm sorry," she murmured.

"I know, hon," he whispered back. "I find it impossible to stay mad at you, but I'm worried."

"I know you are, but can we please table this for now? I'm exhausted." She didn't know how long she could put him off or what she might say to dissuade him. He wasn't the sort of man who would let something like this go forever, especially because his job was to dig around in every possible threat to her life. He had to assume Richard was on that list of possible threats.

The crazy thing was that Tavis was wrong. There was no threat to her life. Richard certainly didn't ransack her apartment. She doubted he even had a clue where she lived. He wouldn't hire people to rough up her place either. Why? That wasn't what he wanted.

Tavis was wasting his time trying to find someone who might be a specific threat to her. The idea was fictional. Her father overreacting. He'd always been this way. Overprotective. Overbearing. Over everything.

Nope. This situation with Richard was personal. He would never hurt her. He simply wanted to marry her and would stop at nothing to ensure she eventually consented.

With no clear answers to anything, Colette finally drifted off to sleep.

CHAPTER 16

Tavis sighed as he rubbed his temples with his free hand. Colette was finally sleeping, her body relaxed against him. She'd cried herself to sleep, worn herself out. He wasn't surprised. She was emotionally drained.

Damn, but he was frustrated. He hadn't been kidding when he'd told her it was impossible to stay angry with her. He had a soft spot for the woman that turned him into a marshmallow, especially when she cried.

Did she think he didn't fully understand what was going on with Richard? The only reason he stopped badgering her was because he doubted there was a single thing she could tell him he didn't already know.

He didn't need to read the previous texts to know that Richard Tillerman was blackmailing her. He was probably trying to be subtle about it, but she wasn't stupid. She knew. That's why she was falling apart.

The reason Tillerman sent her that picture was to prove he'd been following her that night and there were more pictures where that one came from. Or at least he wanted her to believe they existed.

Nope. Tavis didn't need to read a single email to know that Tillerman was so desperate to marry into Colette's family for his own personal benefit that he was going to extreme measures to ensure it happened.

It was impossible to know if the asshole actually had pictures of Colette from later in the evening in a compromising position. But the presumption was that he did. Why else would he be blackmailing her unless he had leverage?

He could ruin her reputation, but more importantly, it would be a living hell for her father if Tillerman released pictures of Colette having sex in the front seat of a truck with a stranger.

The question was what did Colette intend to do about it? Tavis wondered if she would actually consider marrying the asshole to save her father's reputation. Surely not. And how was she going to explain her pregnancy to Tillerman?

Obviously, Tillerman had no idea she was pregnant. The thought hadn't occurred to him. Tavis was beyond furious, but his hands were also tied. He understood perfectly well what Colette was facing. She didn't want Tavis to know the entire story because she feared he would have his team go after Tillerman, which would risk the man releasing the pictures.

She wasn't exactly wrong. What she didn't understand was Tavis would never do anything that would put her in danger, even if that danger was to her reputation or that of her father's. Though Lord knew Tavis found it hard to give a shit about protecting her father.

But William Loughlin was secretary of state in addition to being Colette's father, and Tavis would respect the man out of consideration for that fact alone. Even though Colette was clearly frustrated with the way her parents tried to control her life, she loved them. They were her family. Tavis would be an insensitive dick if he did anything to infuriate her father. Even if the man deserved it.

Were her parents a soft place to fall though? That was the burning question. Would they turn away from her when they found out she was pregnant? Tavis wasn't sure. He doubted Colette was sure.

What Colette didn't realize was that Tavis himself was her soft place. He would be there for her. She might not be ready to face this truth or even consider it. It was going to be an uphill battle convincing her that Tavis didn't care she was pregnant. He'd already fallen hard for her before he'd known that fact. It was too late. She was his, and that baby inside her was too. It didn't matter that he hadn't fathered the child. He was head over heels for the mother, and therefore he would feel the same about her baby. It wasn't even a question. It was simply his truth.

He was trying his best to show her how he felt. She wouldn't be receptive to him telling her yet. He feared if he came on too strong, he would push her away. That was the last thing he wanted.

Colette whimpered in her sleep and snuggled in closer to his side. She did that nearly every night, but this time she slid her knee up higher. When it rubbed against his cock, he sucked in a breath and held it.

Keeping his dick from declaring an all-out revolt lately had been challenging. Tavis felt like he had several private chats a day with his small head, trying to silently explain that his cock needed to be more patient because Colette needed time and time was something they had in abundance. Several months of it.

He did worry she might become less and less inclined to get intimate with him as she began to grow. Her concern was unfounded. He would be attracted to her no matter how big her stomach grew. So far he hadn't seen any evidence the few times he'd gotten a glimpse of her belly lately, but her breasts were another story.

They were larger, and based on the way she winced sometimes, he suspected they were sore. Her bras were probably too small and constricting.

Colette moaned softly as if she were having a frustrating dream, but her knee moved again, and damn…

Tavis tried to control his breathing, his chest rising and falling with every inhale and exhale. He didn't want to wake her. He didn't want her to know how she was affecting him. He remained perfectly still.

How mortifying to be so thoroughly turned on by the woman while she was asleep. Apparently, his cock didn't care. It didn't get the message she wasn't conscious. It only knew she was stroking him.

Suddenly, Colette stiffened. A moment later, her breath hitched and she eased her knee away from his cock.

He let out a hiss, unable to stop it. *Shit.*

Colette's body was rigid next to him. She knew he was awake. She knew he knew she was also awake. All that remained was admitting this fact in the silence.

He waited, wondering if she would speak up or pretend this awkward moment wasn't happening and go back to sleep.

Suddenly, after long moments of nothing but heavy breathing and no other movement, Colette slid her hand down his chest, over his abs, and lower.

He gritted his teeth, uncertain what the fuck to expect, but then she lifted her palm and wrapped her fingers around his erection.

He couldn't breathe. Maybe he had fallen asleep and this was a dream. A damn good dream. One he didn't want to risk waking up from.

She stroked her fist up and down his cock over his shorts. "You don't care, do you?" she whispered, her voice hoarse.

He licked his lips. "Care about what, hon?" He cared about a whole hell of a lot of things. Which thing did she think he *didn't* care about?

"That I'm pregnant. You don't care that I'm carrying another man's child."

He ran his hand down his face. "No, hon. I don't care."

"Is it that you're still attracted to me anyway? Or is it more?"

He opened his mouth to make sure she knew exactly how he felt, but she shook her head, stopping him. "No. Don't answer that question."

He swallowed. It was difficult to answer any question with her fingers wrapped around his length, her grip easing up and down his shaft.

She suddenly released him, but it was temporary. A few moments later, she was dipping her fingers under the waistband of his shorts. A few seconds after that, she had her sweet palm wrapped around his length again, this time skin to skin.

"Colette…" he warned. She was playing with fire.

She responded by scooting down his body and tugging his shorts over his hips, freeing his length.

He gasped when she wrapped her lips around him and sucked him into her mouth without warning. His hands came to her shoulders, but his eyes rolled back in his head and he couldn't find the words to stop her.

He was going to come. This hadn't been in his plans. Not for tonight anyway. Not in the near future at all. And as much as he enjoyed her lips wrapped around his cock, he preferred to take care of his woman before he came.

She was determined and relentless though, bobbing on and off him, her fist wrapped around the base of his cock.

Somehow he managed to find the willpower to haul her off him and drag her up his body.

"Hey," she protested. "Why did you stop me?"

"Because I don't want to come in your mouth, Colette." He tipped her chin back and met her gaze. "If we're going to take this next step, we're not going to half ass it."

She licked her lips. "I thought maybe…"

He drew in a breath. "You thought you could just swallow me and go back to sleep?"

"Well, yeah."

"Why? Do you feel like you owe me a blowjob for some reason?" Part of him was angry because he knew he was right. Part of him was frustrated that she couldn't fully open up to him.

"When you say it like that, it sounds cheap and dirty," she murmured.

"It feels cheap and dirty too, hon. If I'm going to come inside you, the first time is not going to be in your mouth, Colette. Are you ready for me to splay you out naked and ravish you? Because I'd like nothing more than to make you scream my name before I slide into your warmth."

She chewed on the corner of her bottom lip, searching his gaze. "I'm pregnant."

"Yep. Pregnant women do have sex and orgasms," he pointed out.

She swallowed. "My breasts are tender, and I'm going to start growing soon. How long do you think you're going to find me attractive?"

His eyes shot wide. "Until you die, Colette. Don't ask me that again. You're gorgeous, and I'm going to find you just as gorgeous and sexy and attractive when you're nine months pregnant, probably more so."

She gasped, her lips parting in shock.

"I'm not going to wake up one morning and find you repulsive, Colette. It's insulting to insinuate such a thing. Almost as insulting as the pity blowjob you were plotting. Either give me your entire body, or nothing at all. What were you thinking would happen between us? Huh? Did you think you could slide into bed every night for the next seven months, suck me off, and keep your clothes on so I can't see or touch you?"

She blew out a frustrated breath and glanced at his chest. At least she hadn't moved off him. She was still positioned sprawled over the top of him. "I hadn't thought it through, Tavis," she whispered.

"Well, how about you think it through right now. Let me help you out. I have stipulations."

She met his gaze again, biting her lip.

He had her full attention, so he continued. "You can give me as many blowjobs as you want, but every one of them will be preceded with either my mouth or my fingers or my cock inside your pussy. Until you've come, your lips don't come near my dick."

She sucked in a breath. "That's a bit extreme, don't you think?"

He shook his head. "You're not going to slide down my body, suck me off, and go to sleep, Colette. Never. If you've dated anyone that let you do that in the past, he was a dick."

Based on her wince, he had to guess she'd been in such a situation before. Jesus.

"I know you're struggling to believe I care about you, but I do. A lot. I've wanted to worship your body for weeks now. Are you ready for that? Are you ready for me to strip off that T-shirt and panties, spread you open, and make your eyes roll back? Because that's what I'm offering, hon. Everything. And I won't take less than everything."

"It's not that simple, Tavis." She scrambled off him and sat next to him. "I'm fucking pregnant. You can't ignore that. It's not going to go away. I'm going to get huge and ugly and emotional and my life is going to flip upside down. I don't have the luxury of entering into a sweet relationship with anyone, especially not someone who will eventually break my heart."

He bolted to sitting and grabbed her face with both hands. "I'm super clear that you're pregnant, Colette. I'm not ignoring it half as much as you are. And no part of you is ever going to be ugly. You don't have to martyr yourself just because you had unprotected sex one time. Your life isn't over. You absolutely are permitted to enjoy life, fall in love, get married. You're entitled to be worshipped and treated like a queen. I'm just waiting for you to realize that and accept that I don't care if you're pregnant."

She gasped, eyes wide. "You can't seriously mean that."

He continued. "Yes, I can. Does it put a wrench in things? Yes. Mostly for you. But, like I've told you before, I already fell for you before we added this unexpected complication. What if you suddenly found out you had cancer or lost an arm or something? You think I'd turn away?"

She swallowed.

"You do, don't you? You think I'd leave you to deal with a pile of shit on your own. I hate that for you. I hate that you can't trust me to care about you no matter what happens. I hate that you think I would ever do anything to intentionally break your heart."

Tavis hadn't meant for all this to spew out tonight. He hadn't thought she was ready to hear it. He'd feared she would think it was too soon to have deep feelings for another person. Hell, he couldn't be sure she felt the same way about him. But she'd pushed him right over the edge, so they were having this conversation right damn now in the middle of the night.

"I've thought long and hard about this, Colette."

"You should. I'm a mess."

He shook his head. "No. You have it all wrong. I don't care about the parts you think I should care about. What I worry about is upsetting your world more than it already is by inserting myself in it when I'm not from the sort of ilk your parents expect. My concern is that you'll resent me eventually when I don't fit in."

"That's insane. I don't care about what my parents think. Fuck them."

He lifted a brow. "You say that now. What happens when you bring me home? Does your dad embrace me, pat me on the back, and offer me a cigar?"

She winced.

"Yeah, that's what I thought."

"Do *you* care what my father thinks?"

"No. Not a bit. But he's your father, and I totally understand blood. It's powerful. But you need a soft spot to fall and that's me."

"You want to be my soft spot?" she whispered.

"No. I *am* your soft spot. I am that man. I want everything. As long as I can reach out every morning for the rest of my life and feel you next to me, I don't give a fuck about anything else. If you don't feel the same way about me, I'll walk away, Colette. But if you do, don't throw this away like a martyr."

A tear ran down her cheek.

He swiped at it with his thumb and kissed her gently on the lips. He was fucking nervous as hell, uncertain which direction this was going to go. Perhaps he'd put this conversation off in order to avoid her possible response.

When she didn't pull away, he lowered his voice. "If I thought you belonged in your father's world… If I thought it made you happy and that you needed jewelry and fancy clothes and shoes and shit, I wouldn't tear you away from that. I wouldn't even suggest it. I wouldn't be in your bed right now with my cock hanging out, pleading my case."

"Tavis…"

He tapped her lips to silence her. "You told me when we met that there was a mix-up with the stork," he reminded her, offering a slight grin. "I get that. I'm betting you've spent hours imagining a lot of scenarios for when we return to the States. I'd venture to guess that none of those scenarios include your parents welcoming you home with open arms and helping you raise this baby."

She shuddered and shook her head.

"That's what I thought. Which means you've been contemplating quitting school and finding an apartment and becoming a single parent."

She glanced down.

"Why can't you see that I want to fit into one of those scenarios?"

"Because it's too crazy to believe, Tavis."

He shrugged. "And yet…"

She groaned.

"How about you let me decide what's crazy and what's not. How about you let me make love to you and *show* you how I feel." He was tossing the word love around flippantly, never directly saying what he knew he felt in his heart. She might freak out if he used that word so directly at this stage.

He might freak out too. He'd never told a woman he

loved her. He'd never felt this strongly about anyone in his life. And he hadn't even had sex with her.

"I don't have all the answers yet. Mostly because I don't know all the factors. I can't fully predict what your parents are going to say and do when we return. I doubt it will be pretty based on what I know, but it wouldn't be pretty without me in the picture either."

"No. It won't."

"Can you look me in the eyes and tell me you don't want something more with me?"

She met his gaze, sitting up taller. "I want everything with you. You have to know that."

Thank God.

He closed his eyes and slowly smiled. A huge weight lifted off his shoulders.

"Let me show you how I feel. Stop hiding from me. If you still want to give me a blowjob after I've worn you out with my mouth and my cock, I won't stop you." He gave her a goofy grin.

She chuckled. "Do you have to be so rigid about blowjobs? Why can't I sometimes just go down on you? I could wake you up that way."

He smiled broader. "We'll see. Some day. Not today."

She rolled her eyes playfully. "Fine. Be that way. If I let you go first, you'll let me finish what I started?"

He shook his head. "Not a chance. If you let me worship you, I'm coming inside your pussy tonight."

"I think I can live with that. But don't take it as a sign that I totally believe we can have a future together. You have no idea what you're stepping into. My world is fucked up. I'll be squirting gasoline all over the place when I return to the States. Don't even try to make promises about what you intend to do. You can't understand the complexity of the situation."

"I bet I understand more than you give me credit for. If you're talking about Tillerman, I'm not an idiot. I don't need to see those fucking texts you're hiding to piece things together. That man is blackmailing you." He didn't ask. He told her what he knew.

She swallowed hard.

"That picture was a warning. You're worried he has others. You're worried he will release them to the world. You're worried about what it will do to your father's career if he does. I bet you're even hoping you can mollify him for a few months until he sees you and realizes you're pregnant. Then maybe he'll give up the fight because you won't look so appealing to him."

Yeah, a few more tears fell now.

He swiped them away with his thumbs and brought his forehead to hers. "There's no reason to keep things from me or try to bottle them up inside. You're not helping yourself."

Her lip trembled. "You're going to go after him, aren't you?"

"Yes. Already working on it." He didn't hedge. He held her gaze.

More tears fell. "What if he releases the pictures before I return?"

"He won't."

"You can't know that."

"What I do know is that I'm the man in your bed. I'm the man who's going to hold you at night and make you come so hard you can't remember your own name. I'll be damned if I'll let you secretly text some fucking asshole on the side behind my back, letting him think he has a chance with you."

Damn. Tavis hated raising his voice and giving her

ultimatums, but this had gone too far for too long. It was going to get worse if he didn't nip it in the bud.

Would Tillerman release the pictures to the universe? It could happen, but he didn't think the man would take that kind of risk without serious provocation. Tillerman knew good and well that releasing any pics he might have could backfire on him.

"Please let me handle this," he begged.

"Okay," she whispered.

Headway. He'd take it.

CHAPTER 17

Colette's heart was thumping so hard it felt like it would beat right out of her chest. She had misjudged Tavis in a big way. The man knew exactly what was happening. Of course he did. He was intelligent and sharp. She had no idea why she'd thought she could keep the intimate details from him. It had been a losing battle from the start.

"We should get some sleep," he muttered, still cupping her face.

What? Was he serious? Yeah, the conversation had been heavy, but it had also been mixed with sexual inuendo.

Actually, most of their discussion with regard to sex hadn't been inuendo at all. He'd been perfectly frank with her. She'd had her mouth around his erection just a few minutes ago. He'd talked of making her scream before he slid into her. Now he wanted to get some sleep?

She twisted away from him and slid off the side of the bed. After padding to the bathroom, she flipped on the light and looked at herself in the mirror. Her eyes were puffy and red. Dried tear tracks lay pale against her cheeks. She splashed water on her face and patted it dry.

When she turned around to reenter the bedroom, she made a decision. Head held high, renewed purpose in her steps, she came to her side of the bed, stripped off the T-shirt, and wiggled free of her panties.

Tavis watched her every move in the faint light coming from the moon. He rose onto one elbow, facing her as she slid back under the covers.

It had been risky, this decision to put herself out there like this, but it paid off. He didn't hesitate to drag her against his side and lean over to take her lips.

She melted into him in a heartbeat. That's the way it always was when he kissed her. The world ceased to exist around them. It was just the two of them. They had a connection that was undeniable.

He deepened the kiss, angling his head to one side as he slipped his tongue into her mouth. His hand smoothed down to her arm and then her ribcage and finally up to cup her breast.

She moaned, arching into his touch, wordlessly pleading for more.

He licked the seam of her lips and stared at her as his fingers found her nipple. "Is this okay? I know your breasts are tender."

She nodded. "It feels so good. You don't have to be gentle."

"I don't want to hurt you."

"You won't. A little pain won't kill me."

He smirked. "A little pain? You say that like you'd actually appreciate a bit of discomfort." He followed that up with a pinch to her nipple.

She moaned and arched farther. "Yes," she murmured.

He kissed her again but didn't linger. Instead, he nibbled a path down her chin to her chest and kept going until he reached her nipple. Gently, reverently, he flicked his tongue over the tip.

Holy mother.

She grabbed his biceps to steady herself and keep the room from spinning, but when he scraped his teeth over the sensitive tip, she cried out.

"Mmm," he muttered. "You like that." He still held the globe gently, reverently. She didn't know how he read her so well, but she appreciated that he did.

Wetness pooled between her legs, and she restlessly shifted against him.

Tavis released her breast and moved his palm down her body. "Open for me, hon."

She spread her knees wider, shaking. She'd needed this for weeks. The release he was about to give her. It had always been on the table, but she hadn't taken it because she'd been too stubborn. The memory of the one amazing orgasm he'd given her weeks ago before the ceiling fell in on them had taunted her mercilessly. Finally, the waiting was over.

Tavis held her gaze as he dragged his fingers through her slit and then found her clit.

She dug her fingertips into his biceps. He was lucky she didn't keep her nails long or he'd have halfmoon crests on his skin.

Finally, he pushed two fingers slowly into her.

She moaned long and drawn out as he entered her.

"You're so fucking sexy, Colette. You take my breath away."

"Please stop teasing me. I need you inside me," she begged.

He flicked her clit and added a third finger, making her dig her heels into the mattress and lift her ass clear off the bed. "You sure you're ready?" he teased. Damn infuriating man.

"I've been ready for weeks," she gritted out.

He removed his fingers and rolled partly away from her. A second later, he was back, tearing a condom open with his teeth before sheathing himself in seconds.

She obviously couldn't get pregnant, but that didn't mean she hadn't picked up anything else from her one-night stand. And she and Tavis hadn't discussed his history either. This was the responsible thing to do. If they were going to move into a new phase in their relationship though, she wanted to see a doctor and get checked out so they could lose the condoms.

She expected him to climb between her legs, but he rarely did the expected. Instead, he leaned forward and kissed her nipple again. "So restless," he murmured.

"Tavis..." She tried to make her voice sound forceful, but she suspected she'd failed and just sounded desperate.

Apparently, pregnancy was not affecting her libido. She'd known that of course because she'd been restless and needy every time he'd touched her or held her. But it was blatantly obvious now.

He took his sweet time kissing her nipples back and forth until they were stiff points and she couldn't lie still. Finally, he lifted a knee and nestled it between hers. She held her breath, willing him to shift the rest of his body between her thighs. She even opened them wider to encourage or invite him.

"You're so impatient," he teased as he shifted the rest of his body into position and lined his cock up with her channel.

She'd never felt this level of arousal before. Not with anyone. Granted, she'd also never had this emotional connection with another man either. She'd simply had sex sometimes. It hadn't caused the rafters to shake.

She glanced up at the literal rafters above them as if she might find them trembling from the sexual tension in the room.

Tavis kissed her again, consuming her, forcing her to shift all of her attention to his mouth and tongue.

She did, dueling with him, her hands on his waist now as she simultaneously tried to lift her hips upward.

Tavis released her mouth, met her gaze, and thrust forward. He gave her exactly what she craved, filling her completely all at once. No easing into her.

She moaned so loud she feared someone in another cabin might hear her. After all, there were no glass windows, just screens. She could only hope the cabins were far enough apart that no one would catch the sound of her voice.

"Don't worry about the neighbors, hon. Focus on me."

She jerked her gaze to his, realizing she'd been staring at the windows while she adjusted to his thick shaft. She was restless now. She needed him to move. And she wiggled her hips against his to make her point.

He held her gaze as he eased out and then thrust back in deeper, taking her breath away.

"Jesus, you're gorgeous," he whispered. "Do that again." He pulled almost out and thrust in a third time, tilting his pelvis enough to make her eyes roll back.

Suddenly, he changed the pace, picking up speed. His hands slid under her to grip her shoulders from behind and keep her from slamming into the headboard.

Was it possible he might be able to make her come like this? From sex alone? She never would have believed it, but she was so close. The only friction she was getting against her clit was from the base of his cock with each pass, and still her arousal was climbing.

"Tavis," she cried out.

"I'm right here, hon. Come for me."

She tipped her head back, all of her focus on how damn good he made her feel. Her breasts were heavier than normal, her nipples hard as rocks and so sensitive every time his chest grazed over the tips. Maybe pregnancy made her hornier than usual.

Tavis released one shoulder to slide his hand down between them and find her clit. The moment his fingers rubbed the bundle of nerves, she dug her heels into the mattress and groaned.

Seconds later, she came, her channel gripping him tightly, pulsing hard around his shaft. Stars floated around the edges of her vision. Her body shuddered every few seconds, completely out of her control.

Tavis held steady for a moment and then pumped a few more times, growling out his own release before finally holding himself deeply embedded inside her and dropping his forehead to hers.

He was panting. So was she.

He was also smiling.

"Cocky, are we?" she asked.

"Yes. I'm two for two. For a woman who hasn't ever had an orgasm with a man, I'd say I'm doing okay."

She rolled her eyes and slid her hands around to squeeze his fine ass. "Okay is an understatement. I stand by what I said last time. I'm ruined for all other men."

"And like I said last time you came for me, you're mine anyway, so I'm glad you're ruined for other men."

She stared at him, beginning to believe him.

He shrugged. "I know you still doubt me, but I'll prove myself to you. I have months to convince you. I bet if I make you come like that at least once or twice a day for the rest of our time in Uganda, you'll find it hard to walk away from me." His expression was soft, his eyes dancing.

She smoothed her hands up to his face and held his gaze. "Tavis, it was never going to be easy to walk away from you. Not from the first night when you picked me up. I knew I was in trouble when you carried my suitcase. I knew it when you lowered the mosquito net around my bed to keep me safe. I knew it when you spent the rest of the night researching my profession. No man has ever taken an interest in what I do. Never."

His expression was serious. "Then don't. Don't walk away from me. Stop entertaining the idea."

She licked her lips. "You say that now, but..."

He shook his head. "No buts. Just you and me. We can do this."

"I want to believe you, but when you meet my father..."

"What? Have I ever given you the impression I would cower to anyone?"

"No." He hadn't. But he hadn't faced off with Secretary Loughlin yet. She glanced away.

"Colette, here's what I need you to know. I'm here for you until you tell me to get lost. If you can't take the pressure from your parents and kick me to the curb, that's when I'm gone. I'll do everything in my power to be polite and courteous and respectful to your parents, except let them treat you badly. That's where I draw the line. I don't care what they think about me or how they talk to me or even if they dismiss me. That's on them. What I care about is how they treat you and that you know you have me at your back."

Her chest tightened. No one had ever been so fully on her side. No one had ever stood up for her or faced off with her parents for her. She had very little doubt now that

Tavis could and would. Head high. Shoulders back. Gaze firm.

"You with me, Colette?"

"Yes." She was. She wanted to be, so she was. She knew doubts would seep in from time to time over the coming months, but all she had to do was look him in the eyes and she would be reminded that he was on her team.

CHAPTER 18

Nothing in the world could compare to seeing gorillas up close in their own habitat. They were so majestic and strong and powerful. Colette wouldn't even let herself blink while they watched the amazing creatures chow down on leaves in the Bwindi Impenetrable Forest.

The trek to get to them had been hard work. There were no paths, just the natural habitat. A guide with a machete hacked away in front of them to make a space for them to pass, but other than that, they were basically climbing through untouched rainforest.

Colette was exhausted and exhilarated at the same time when they returned to the lodge. After an amazing massage and dinner, she couldn't keep her eyes open.

Tavis read her well, whisking her off to their cabin even before the sun was fully down. He took her into the bathroom, filled the tub with warm water, stripped her out of her clothes, and helped her into the luxurious bath.

After a thirty-minute soak, he helped her out, dried her off, pulled one of his T-shirts over her head, and tucked her into bed. When he climbed in next to her, she snuggled up to his side and promptly fell asleep while he caught up on his emails.

It seemed like moments before Colette woke up to the feel of Tavis's fingers training over her hip. She was shocked when she blinked her eyes open to find the room filled with daylight. "Shit. How long did I sleep?"

"About ten hours. Without moving. I had to pull my arm out from under your head for a while when the circulation cut off to my fingers," he joked. "If you hadn't been plastered against me, your breaths hitting my pecs, your chest rising and falling, I might have thought you were no longer living."

She swatted at him playfully. "I was tired."

He tipped her chin back and kissed her. "Tracking gorillas was hard work."

"I'm always tired."

He nodded. "Growing another human inside you is also hard work."

She groaned. For a moment, she'd forgotten she was pregnant. A blissful moment that went up in smoke when reminded.

"Hey? You okay?" he asked. "I didn't mean to upset you."

She dropped her head back against his chest, her fingers dancing over his muscles. "It's okay. I just…try not to think about it."

He stroked her hair, not saying anything for a few moments. Finally, he cleared his throat. "I'm worried about you. You cringe every time you let yourself think about this baby. Every time I bring it up you look away and change the subject. You have options, you know. No one is going to make you keep a baby if you don't want to."

She inhaled long and slow. He was right, but she couldn't picture going through with either of the most reasonable options. Abortion was out of the question. Not that she would make that choice for someone else, but now that she was pregnant, she simply couldn't do it herself. There was a human inside her.

And adoption? It wasn't as if she hadn't pondered that many times too. If she went home six months pregnant and announced she was giving this baby up for adoption, her parents would probably disown her and have a coronary. They might anyway.

Tavis continued to stroke her hair. He wasn't going to make this decision for her. He wasn't going to pressure her in any way. He was just going to be his usual supportive self until he started oozing sugar.

She looked at him. "I try to visualize every scenario and all of them make my skin crawl. Abortion makes me feel like vomiting. The thought of carrying a baby to term and then handing it to someone else isn't much better. But I'm also scared about how I might feel about keeping it too. This baby deserves more than I have to offer, and what if I resent him or her for intruding on my life?"

He threaded his fingers in her hair and kissed her forehead before responding. "All of those feelings are legitimate. The only plan that has a ticking time clock is the first one. If that's off the table, you don't have to make any other decisions right now. Don't let the future make you sick. We'll cross that bridge when we come to it."

"I'm not sure how many options I'll even have if I return home six months pregnant. My parents will pressure me."

He sighed. "There *is* another option. If you really wanted to, you could not go home at all until after it was born. It's only three months longer than you planned to stay. I'm not sure I'd recommend staying in Uganda to deliver, but we could go somewhere else. You could either return home holding a baby that's far too late to deny or having given it up for adoption without anyone ever knowing."

She stared at him. She hadn't thought of that possibility. "Do you have an answer for everything?"

"No. But if I don't have one, I'll ask someone else." He winked.

"So your plan is to distract me by entertaining me with safaris and gorgeous views and fantastic sex for the next several months?"

"Yep. Is it working?"

"Yes." She rolled her eyes and then narrowed them. "But you're spoiling me, and I'm going to expect this kind of treatment forever."

"Excellent. That's the plan. And why would I stop spoiling you? I'll never have the kind of wealth you're used to, but I'll do everything in my power to make sure you're comfortable and happy."

"You do realize I abhor money, so living a normal life sounds like heaven to me. Think we could get people to stop recognizing me or caring who I'm related to?" Wouldn't that be nice.

"Not sure I can promise that, but I can try."

She lowered her head back to his chest. It unnerved her when they discussed the future as if it were a forgone conclusion that they would be together after her work in Africa was done. It was anything but a forgone conclusion. She was convinced Tavis didn't have the first clue what he was signing up for.

When her phone vibrated on the bedside table, she winced, stiffening. Every time she heard that sound, she flinched. Not every text was from Richard, but often they were. She didn't have a lot of friends who kept in touch with her overseas.

She started to roll away from Tavis, but he hugged her

closer and kissed the top of her head. "May I please look first?"

Colette hesitated. Why bother hiding the truth from Tavis? He'd guessed the entire saga anyway. Finally, she nodded.

He reached over the top of her to snag the phone. "What's your passcode, hon?"

"4613." What did it say about the level of a relationship if your man knew your passcodes?

A few seconds later, Tavis drew in a long breath.

"Do I dare look?"

He held it out in front of her. There was one text that had followed last night's picture.

That's it? No comment?

And then he'd added a second picture from later in the evening. One where she'd been at the bar leaning close to the bartender to be heard over the din. Her skirt was short, almost too short from this angle. Her hair was down but kind of wild from dancing and drinking too much.

"When was that one taken?" Tavis asked.

"Later than the first one."

"So, we have to assume he at least took some sort of incriminating pictures of you, and he intends to taunt you with progressively later pictures with each text."

"It would appear that way." She groaned.

"Did anything happen between you and the, uh, man you hooked up with inside the bar? Anything he might think is enough evidence?"

"Does it matter?"

"Yes. There's a big difference between him taking photos of you dancing with a stranger who could have been your date for all he knew and him following you outside to take pictures of you in the guy's tru—"

When Tavis cut himself off, Colette prompted, "What?"

"Surveillance cameras. I bet the bar had surveillance cameras in the parking lot."

She rose onto her elbow. "I'm not sure I want to find that out."

"Why not? Maybe we can see if Tillerman followed you."

"And maybe you can see the man I was with too clearly for comfort. And maybe you can figure out who he is. And maybe you can see his license plates," she pointed out.

Tavis nodded slowly. "Okay, you have a point. But it's also possible Tillerman has pictures of him that are clear as day too. If he does, and he sends them to you, facial recognition software could nail down his identity in seconds."

She sighed. "And I assume you have access to such software."

"Of course."

She pushed to sitting. "The only nightmare scenario I can possibly come up with that would make my life more complicated and insane would be if you figured out who the hell I fucked in that truck during my lack of good judgment. Can you imagine? Then what? We hunt him down and tell him he has a kid and I share custody with a total stranger?" Her voice rose as she grew more alarmed.

Tavis grabbed her hand and held it. "Okay, I see your point. I will raise you one of my own. The man does have a right to know he has a kid if there's any possible way we could find him. I would be furious if I found out I had a kid wandering around and no one told me. Eventually, this child will do some kind of ancestry report and find his or her dad."

Colette chewed on her bottom lip. He was right. And fuck, things *could* get worse. "Fine. Have your people look at the surveillance cameras." She jerked her hand out of his, rolled off the bed, and hurried to the bathroom. She didn't have morning sickness yet today, but she still might vomit anyway.

After a quick shower and putting on clean clothes, Colette returned to the sitting area of the cabin to find Tavis on the phone. He immediately put it on speaker and set it in front of him on the coffee table, reaching for her to join him. "Ajax, I put you on speaker. Colette is with me now."

"Nice to meet you, Colette."

"You too, Ajax." She took a seat next to Tavis, rubbing her hands on her khaki pants.

"Let me fill you in on what I was just telling Bones."

"Bones?" She glanced at him, lifting a brow.

"That's the nickname the guys call me."

"Why?" She glanced up and down his frame. "It's not like you're too skinny."

Ajax chuckled. "That's for sure. The man sitting next to you is a beast. Twice during BUD/S training he broke an instructor's arm. He earned the nickname fair and square."

Tavis rolled his eyes. "Thanks, Ajax. Let's maybe put that on a billboard."

"Oh, good idea," Ajax joked.

Colette grinned at Tavis. For some reason she enjoyed knowing at one point in his life for a brief moment he'd had a weakness.

"Can we be serious here?" Tavis said, talking to the phone.

"Of course," Ajax responded. "I was telling Tavis that we've been looking for Steve Lacoste, and it turns out there's a good chance he's actually in Africa."

Colette's spine stiffened. "Are you serious?" She glanced at Tavis. She'd never suspected Steve Lacoste for a second. She'd known Tavis and his team were turning over every leaf, but Steve? It had been a long time since she'd given him the slip, and she'd never seen or heard from him again.

Tavis set his hand on top of hers over her thigh and spoke toward the phone. "Is there any chance Secretary Loughlin is aware of that fact?"

"Hard to say, but if he is it would explain a lot. On the other hand, if he is, why the hell did he let Colette leave the country? And why keep this knowledge to himself?"

Colette winced. "He wasn't fond of me leaving the country. Tried to talk me out of it about a dozen times, including the night before I left the States." *Which was why I was out drinking and got myself knocked up.* But she wasn't going to say that to Ajax.

"Can you think of any reason why your father would have been either in contact with Mr. Lacoste or have knowledge of his whereabouts?"

"No. Nothing. He's never mentioned that name again since he fired him. As far as I know, my father never even knew the man was hitting on me. He fired him for losing me for two weeks."

"Right. Then we have to assume either he *did* know something, or he had everyone who ever worked for you followed just to keep tabs on them."

Colette couldn't believe this was happening. "Anything is possible," she consented. "But he's had detail on me that goes back years. I still think he's just paranoid."

"Could be," Tavis agreed, "but my gut tells me otherwise."

"Not gonna lie, Colette," Ajax added. "I have to agree with Tavis on this one. Something doesn't feel right."

"Okay, let's assume for a moment that someone is

tracking me. Why would they follow me all the way to Uganda? They could have snatched me in the States easier."

Tavis shook his head. "Not really. It would be much easier to kidnap you while you're in a rather corrupt country. Then they could hold you for ransom and your father wouldn't even have the use of the CIA to help find you."

Colette licked her lips. "Well, there's no way Richard Tillerman could be a suspect then. My father loves him. He'd pay the guy to come over here and drag me home. He'd probably chuckle if that asshole kidnapped me to attain his goal of marrying up."

"She has a point," Ajax agreed.

Tavis leaned back in his seat and rubbed his forehead. She'd learned this was what he did when he was thinking. "I hate to say this out loud, but there could be more than one person who'd like to get their hands on Colette." He stiffened, his other hand gripping hers too tightly, though she doubted he realized it.

"Forgive me," Colette said, "but can we back up this train for a moment. I'm not buying that my father has anything to do with me being in danger. He's domineering and important and can pull a lot of weight when he needs to, but I know he loves me. So does my mom. They might have a funny way of showing it, but my father would never willingly endanger my life. If he knew Steve Lacoste was following me, he would have half the state department on the guy's tail."

"Who says he doesn't?" Tavis raised this question.

Colette swiped her hand over her face. He had a point, but she still found it unlikely. "I feel like we're on a wild goose chase. We don't know anyone wishes me harm," she reminded them, glancing at Tavis. Obviously, Tillerman was a possible exception for completely different reasons.

"I hear you, Colette," Ajax stated. "And I don't want you to be constantly looking over your shoulder. I promise whether or not someone is following you, you're in good hands. Nothing will happen to you while Tavis is on the clock."

"I believe that." She leaned her head on his shoulder.

"Good. Now, I'm going to track down Steve Lacoste because I want to know where the hell he is, and I'm going to get my hands on the footage from the security cameras at the bar you went to the night before you left the States."

"Could you please keep whatever you find to yourself?" Colette implored.

"Absolutely. I'll call you if I find anything."

"Thank you." Tavis ended the connection and wrapped his arms around Colette. "Put it out of your mind for now. Let's go see some hippos."

She chuckled. "I like that plan."

CHAPTER 19

Even with the interruptions and the extra problems piled on Colette's lap, Tavis thought the trip did her a world of good. By the time they returned to the apartment on Sunday, she was smiling more and walking lighter on her feet.

He'd like to think his cock had something to do with her shift in mood, and maybe it did. He certainly hadn't stopped making love to her. As promised, he made her come at least once a day, usually twice. Sometimes he was inside her early in the morning or late at night. Sometimes he woke her up with his mouth on her.

He loved the way she gripped him when she was out of her mind with arousal. She either dug her nails into his arms or pulled on his hair when he had his head between her legs. It was fucking hot.

The morning sickness stayed at bay, thank God. It could have lasted through the entire first trimester. Instead, it seemed to have dissipated significantly.

She wasn't the only one smiling. He couldn't stop

grinning either. He felt like they'd leaped over an enormous hurdle together. They were more cohesive. He doubted she believed he would stay with her, but he had plenty of time to prove he was in this for the long haul.

They settled into a new routine, one where they didn't have to tiptoe around the elephant in the room—sexual attraction. It was so much easier climbing into bed with her, knowing she wouldn't shut him out. It was easier knowing he could walk in on her in the bathroom, join her in the shower, hold her the few times she got sick.

He loved to wash her hair, run his fingers through it while she moaned in appreciation. He loved to surprise her by suddenly sitting her on the counter in the kitchen or the bathroom and thrusting his tongue into her pussy.

If he lived to be a thousand, he would still get a hard-on from the memory of her moaning in pleasure.

A week after they returned to Kampala, Ryker and Ajax located Steve Lacoste in Ethiopia. The man was working for a diplomat as his protection detail. He was apparently undercover, which explained why they hadn't easily found him.

Ryker couldn't spare the resources to keep someone on Richard Tillerman at all times, and none of them could see the point anyway. The man was still going to work every day and living his life in the States. Following him wouldn't change the fact that he got a kick out of tormenting Colette with another picture every few days. It would seem the man took thousands that night. Some of his shots were only seconds after the previous one he'd sent.

Colette hadn't responded to a single text, but she had badgered Tavis about doing so. It didn't sit right with him. He hated the idea of his woman letting another man believe she would be coming home to him at Christmas.

Of course, Tavis couldn't tell her what to do. Maybe she would dump his ass the moment they touched down on American soil. That seemed increasingly unlikely, but they were definitely living in a bubble. This wasn't the real world.

In this world, Colette was his. The baby was his. She wouldn't be able to hide her belly forever. Soon it would grow round, and if her classmates noticed, they would believe Tavis was the father. Why wouldn't they? He was her boyfriend as far as they were concerned.

Colette didn't want anyone to find out, and she intended to go to great lengths to see that they didn't, which was her prerogative. She was particularly concerned that if anyone found out, it would somehow get back to her father. The world could become very small very quickly. Right now, the only people who knew she was pregnant were Tavis and the doctor at the campus clinic.

It was Saturday. She'd spent the morning in the library, and now they were waiting on a call from Ryker with information about the security cameras at the bar.

Colette nearly jumped out of her chair when the phone buzzed, and he held her hand tightly in his as he connected and put them on speaker phone. "Ryker. You have me and Colette."

"Oh, good. Hi, Colette."

"Hi, Ryker."

"What have you got?" Tavis didn't want to beat around the bush.

"Can you open your laptop while we're on the phone? I'm sending you some pictures."

"It's open already." Tavis had thought this might happen. If Ryker had anything, he would forward it. "And...there's the email now." He kept his grip on Colette's hand while he used the mouse to open the email. There was a zip file, and he glanced at Colette while it opened.

She was breathing deeply, probably trying to keep from panicking, and she pressed their combined hands against her thigh.

When the file opened and the pictures popped up, she gasped. "Jesus."

"Yeah, they had really good security cameras at that bar. And we're lucky they were backed up. This footage could have been deleted. I have a few hours of video, but I took several screenshots for now," Ryker informed them.

Some of the pictures were blurry or far away, but as Tavis scrolled through them, a few were clearer. Colette's leg started bouncing. He could feel her pulse racing in her wrist.

When he glanced at her again, she was white and he worried she might bolt for the bathroom. "Want to keep going?"

She nodded.

He scrolled through a few more. She was stumbling drunk, hanging onto the arm of a man who was also very drunk. There was no reason to ask if this was the man. In addition, there were enough clear shots that Ryker had probably already identified him.

Eventually, they switched to the camera in the parking lot, and Tavis gritted his teeth as he watched the amazing woman he considered his world head toward a truck where her life had changed forever.

Tavis's heart was racing, but he didn't want Colette to see him sweating. He needed to be strong. She was in a full panic.

"Fuck," she muttered.

Ryker had remained quiet for all this time, but he

finally spoke up. "Tavis, you got her? Because she's not going to like what I have to say next."

Colette started crying. Her entire body was shaking as silent tears fell down her cheeks. Ryker couldn't know how gut-wrenching this was. He didn't know she was pregnant.

Tavis pulled her chair closer to his and wrapped an arm around her. His mind went in ten thousand directions all at once. Maybe this guy was someone important. Would he want joint custody if he found out about the baby? What a clusterfuck. How had things gone from fucking bad to worse? Colette could not catch a break.

"Go ahead," Tavis said.

"His name was Joseph Rhineheart. Twenty-four years old. He was out that night with his friends celebrating a birthday."

"Okay." Tavis didn't like the tone of Ryker's voice.

"He wrapped his truck around a pole two hours later and died instantly."

Colette gasped.

Tavis had to hold her up or she would have fallen out of the chair. "Hang on a second, Ryker."

"Take your time. Why don't you call me back?"

"Thank you." Tavis didn't even reach over to end the call. Ryker did it. Instead, Tavis stood, lifted Colette in his arms, and carried her to the sofa where he sat, holding her in his lap, hugging her as tightly as possible while she cried.

There were no words. What did one say in a situation like this? All he could do was comfort her as best as possible. They'd both considered the fact that there was a chance Ryker would find the footage and identify the man, but neither of them could have predicted the man would no longer be living.

She cried for a long time, sobbing mostly until she was completely spent and sat limply in his lap. "I'm sorry."

"Hon… You have no reason to be sorry."

She tipped her head back and offered him a wan smile. "I keep crying. All I do is cry. I just didn't expect… Well, that."

"I know. And I would expect it to be upsetting. Even though you didn't know him, not even his name, it's shocking."

"What if he has family? People are grieving his loss and I'm carrying his child." She rubbed her temples. Her head was probably pounding.

"You don't have to make any decisions about that right now, hon. It's overwhelming."

"Ryker must think I'm crazy. Why would I break down crying like this to find out some guy I fucked behind a bar died later?"

"Because you're human and kind and caring and you would have cried if you'd heard that news even if he hadn't left you with a gift. I would be shook up if I heard someone I slept with died later that night."

"Why the fuck did he drive? He was as drunk as me. I was so wasted that I didn't remember enough about him to describe him or even his name and I knew better than to drive."

"I don't know, hon. People drive drunk. It happens."

She sat up straighter and grabbed Tavis's hand. "I didn't leave him in that car driving away. I swear. We both went back inside. I saw him five minutes later in line for the bathroom."

He cupped her face. "It's not your fault, Colette."

She nodded slowly. "I know. But still…"

"He was probably still at the bar after you left. Ryker said the accident happened two hours later."

Colette drew in a deep breath and rubbed her temples again. "I feel like my life is spinning out of control."

He pulled her against his chest. "It is a bit rocky. Not gonna lie. But I've got you. You're going to live through this awkward stage of life and be fine. I promise."

"It doesn't feel like it right now. What the fuck is going to happen next? A truck is going to plow through the front of my apartment? Food poisoning puts me in the hospital?"

She was rambling, but damn, she had every right to feel out of control. Life was dumping on her daily.

Tavis stood and carried Colette up the stairs and into her bedroom. He pulled back the covers and deposited her on the bed. "Why don't you take a nap."

She rolled onto her back and stared at him. "I have so much to do. My research is falling behind. I shouldn't have taken a week off. And part of me wonders why I'm even bothering. I'm never going to be able to finish my PhD. This entire semester is a farce."

He sat next to her and cupped her face. "It's not. You're going to finish your PhD. Look at me."

Her eyes were wild, but she finally met his gaze. He liked to think it helped ground her when she looked him in the eye. "We've got this. Together."

She blinked at him.

"Take a deep breath and let it out slowly."

At least she did that.

"Good. Again."

Her body relaxed marginally as she exhaled.

"Close your eyes. Let yourself relax. I'm going to call Ryker back. He's probably wondering what happened to us."

Colette rolled onto her side. "Go. Call him. I'll be fine."

Would she? Tavis wasn't sure. He had to hope so.

He jogged back downstairs and returned the call.

"Everything okay?" Ryker asked as a greeting.

"Yeah. That was just a blow."

"I would expect someone to be shocked and startled, but you said she didn't even know the guy. It was a one-night stand."

Tavis dropped onto the couch. "She's stressed and tired," he said, hoping Ryker would drop it. "Please tell me what you know about Tillerman."

"Man's a tool. Cocky bastard. I personally went to see him, watched him come and go from his office lobby. No wonder she doesn't like him."

"Yeah. He's a gem. Based on the photos you were able to get from the security cameras, I imagine he has some rather scandalous pictures of Colette that he obviously snapped all evening long."

"Do you think he followed her and took the pictures for the purpose of later blackmailing her?" Ryker asked.

"Who knows? He might have followed her hoping to casually run into her, which got thwarted and pissed him off when she started flirting with another man."

"The blackmailing was probably an afterthought, though I do not understand why. There are millions of women on this planet. Who would want to marry someone who isn't even interested in them? I can't imagine being that desperate to make a connection with someone's father that I would marry a woman I didn't like. Or worse, one who didn't like me."

"It's mind-boggling. That's for sure. The man must really have a hard-on for her father. It also seems unlikely her father is aware of any of this because the man is still hounding her to give Tillerman a chance."

"Good point. I doubt he knows. What about you? How are things between the two of you?" Ryker asked.

Tavis smiled. In spite of all their problems, he and

Colette were on the same page. "If I had my way, I'd convince her to marry me and move to another country without ever returning to the States at all."

"Wow. That's pretty serious."

"Very," he admitted.

"And she agrees?"

"She's worried. Rightfully so. I get it. She thinks we're living in a bubble, which we are, and that I won't be able to take the heat when we get back and face her parents." *For so many more reasons than I can possibly tell you.*

Ryker chuckled. "She doesn't know you very well if she thinks you can't stand up to her father. Wouldn't matter if he was president of the United States. You'd never let him walk all over you or his own daughter."

Tavis smiled. There wasn't much to smile about at the moment, but Ryker was right.

"Are you sure she's not more worried about herself and her ability to go to her parents with a stiff spine and tell them she's in love with a lowlife Navy SEAL?" He laughed.

"I'm not sure what to think. It's hard to speculate."

"But you're in love with her." It wasn't a question.

"Yeah. I am."

"Have you told her?"

"Not in those words. I don't want her to panic and run, and don't lecture me about how long I've known her," he warned.

"*Me?* Have you forgotten how I met Xena and how fast I made her mine?"

Tavis chuckled. "You're right. I've spent two months with Colette. Nearly every waking hour. It's like our relationship went on fast track."

"I hope you're squeezing in plenty of sleeping hours too," he teased.

"I'll never kiss and tell." Tavis winced quietly. "And on

that note, I need to go check on Colette. I'll talk to you later."

"Sounds good. Later." Ryker broke the connection.

The guys were going to drop their jaws when they found out Colette was pregnant. Not just Ryker and Ajax. All the guys. The entire SEAL team.

Gramps, Keebler, Pitbull, Viper, and Loki rounded out their crew. After the rigged mission they'd been on over a year ago in which six of them ended up in captivity for three months while Ajax and Ryker returned to Ethiopia to rescue them, they were tight. They'd gone into business together. Opened the Holt Agency.

And now? Jesus. Had it really been a year? The past few weeks seemed like months. Tavis was so deeply into the woman resting upstairs that he probably wasn't even thinking rationally.

What the hell were they going to do when they returned? She needed to go back to Johns Hopkins and finish her PhD. He couldn't return to Indiana and leave her alone. He needed to go with her. Hell, he needed to become a stay-at-home dad for a while so she could finish her classes and her dissertation.

A dad... Jesus. How was he going to be a dad in seven short months? Sometimes when it was late at night and Colette was asleep, he would rest his hand on her abdomen and stroke her skin. There was a human in there. A tiny being he intended to raise as his own.

Suddenly, he realized something he'd never fully thought about before. The baby... No one needed to know it wasn't his. Joseph Rhineheart looked enough like Tavis that the baby wouldn't raise suspicions.

Colette had gotten pregnant hours before meeting Tavis. *Hours*. Not days or weeks. By the time they returned to the States, she would be far enough along that people would think, wow, the two of them got together fast, but they wouldn't realize it hadn't been that way.

He'd take shit for it, especially from her father. The man would lose his ever-loving mind when he found out the guy he'd been paying to keep his daughter safe had been sleeping with her the entire time. A man who wasn't in politics. Had no connection to anyone wealthy. A man who had been a Navy SEAL. But Tavis would bet money her father would think that was beneath his only daughter.

The plan had a lot of holes in it. People were going to be furious. He doubted Ajax and Ryker would be shocked by his commitment to Colette, but they were going to be disappointed to lose him because Tavis was moving to Baltimore. But her parents and their social circle... That was going to be a hotbed of contention.

Tavis started pacing as the picture became clearer. Clear as day. That baby was his. No one needed to know otherwise.

It was perfect for Colette. It would take the heat off her. Everyone would blame Tavis instead of Colette. She wouldn't have to tell anyone she'd had unprotected sex with a man she didn't know in a drunken night of defiance.

It could work. It *would* work. Now...when should he tell Colette? Not yet. That was for sure. She wouldn't entertain the idea for one second right now. But in a few months...

There was one possible flaw in his plan: Richard Tillerman. If the man had pics of her in a compromising position behind the bar... But that didn't mean anything. It didn't mean Tavis wasn't the father of the baby. Richard might speculate, but he wouldn't know for sure.

It was settled. At least in Tavis's mind. They would get an apartment with at least two bedrooms near campus. He would stay home with the baby while she finished her

PhD. Afterward, they would move wherever she needed to go. When the baby got a bit older, they could arrange daycare and Tavis could go back to work for the Holt Agency. He was certain he could take a leave of absence and not be cut off for good. Those guys were his brothers. It wouldn't matter where Tavis was living. Hell, he could cut back on his assignments to fit Colette's schedule.

CHAPTER 20

Three months later...

"Slow down, hon. I promise you're not going to be late." Tavis tried not to chuckle as Colette rushed around the apartment, grabbing things and sticking them in her backpack.

He was fairly certain the pregnancy hormones had caused this daily frenzy. She hadn't been this frantic when he'd first met her, but as the weeks went by, she'd taken on this urgency, always worried she would be late getting to campus. They never were. He always got her there on time.

"Have you seen my laptop?" She spun around the room in circles.

Tavis set the last dish he'd been washing from breakfast in the drainer and came to her. He grabbed her around the waist and pulled her into his arms. She didn't fit as well as she used to. Her belly was growing larger. But he could still wrap his arms around her and hold her tight to help her relax.

He brushed the hair from her face. "It's in your backpack already. I put it in there last night after you went to bed."

"You're sure?" She looked skeptical, her eyes narrowed.

"Well, it's kinda big. You can take a glance and see it easily enough. It's not an eraser."

"Oh. Right." She sighed and dropped her forehead to his chest, her hands gripping his belt loops. "I'm sorry. I get kinda crazy. I don't know why."

"It's okay. I happen to like you kinda crazy." He lifted her chin, his heart beating. *Now. Do it now. This is your moment. The perfect segue.* "I happen to love you kinda crazy."

She licked her lips. "Yeah?"

"I happen to love you, Colette. I love you. I've been in love with you for a long time."

A slow smile spread across her face. "Why didn't you say something?" She swatted at his chest.

He chuckled. "I was afraid you weren't ready to hear it, and you might take a step back."

"I might not have been ready to hear it as far back as you felt it, but I've been ready for a while. I love you too."

He grinned. "Yeah?" he said, repeating her word.

"Yep."

He turned her around so the table was behind her and then grabbed her waist and lifted her off the floor.

She squealed as he set her on the table. "*Tavis.*" She swatted at his shoulders. "You have to stop lifting me. I'm too heavy."

He rolled his eyes. They'd had this conversation far too many times. "You've put on about eight pounds, hon. Eight. Not enough."

"I'm fine. The doctor says that happens sometimes. He's not worried."

"Okay, but don't worry about me lifting you either." He slid his hands to her belly and cupped it before easing them up under her shirt to palm her full breasts. They weren't tender anymore. But they were growing. He loved nuzzling them. And he wanted to do so right now.

When he swept her shirt over her head, she protested. "We have to leave soon."

He kissed the upper swell of her breast. "We need to leave in about forty-five minutes, hon. Plenty of time for me to make you come and still gather your belongings." All of which were already in her backpack because he'd made sure last night. He did so every night to avoid this frenzy every morning. The frenzy happened anyway.

He didn't complain, mostly because it was comically cute. He also didn't laugh because he enjoyed staying alive.

She moaned as he reached under the edge of her bra and flicked his tongue over her swollen nipple. While she had her head tipped back, her backpack forgotten, he unfastened her bra and tossed it aside so he could get his mouth around her nipples.

The woman loved it when he sucked her nipples. It drove her wild and caused her to forget whatever she'd been stressing about. As soon as he was certain she was gone for him, he leaned her onto her back on the table and slid his hands down to the waistband of her maternity jeans.

They'd ordered several pairs of pants online when she could no longer button her own. She wore baggy shirts and sweaters at school, so no one had noticed she was pregnant yet, or if they suspected, no one had had the balls to say anything.

Tavis eased the jeans down her legs and off her body, stripping her of the clothes she'd just put on ten minutes ago. He'd also made her come before she'd gotten out of bed this morning, but now he needed her.

He kissed his way from her breasts to her tummy, lingering over the pooch that was growing more and more difficult to hide. She was the most beautiful person on Earth.

"Tavis…" She squirmed, reaching for him. It was amazing how he could make her forget they needed to be anywhere.

He found her clit with his fingers and flicked it over and over while he watched her eyes roll back and her hands fist at her sides. Pregnancy hormones were not lowering his woman's libido. If anything, she was hornier now than she had been when he'd first met her.

She reached for him. "Need you. Stop teasing."

He grinned before unbuttoning his jeans and lowering the zipper. Two seconds later, he was at her entrance, his cock so hard it was impossible to believe he'd had sex with her just last night.

"*Tavis*," she shouted. "Now."

He grabbed her hips and thrust into her, forcing unintelligible sounds from her lips. Sounds that drove him higher and made him pump into her faster. It had taken him weeks to allow himself to fuck her like this. Raw, fast, hard, primal. But she liked it. She begged for it sometimes. And who was he to argue?

What he wouldn't do was leave her hanging. And that included now. He reached between them, circled her clit, and then pinched it.

"Oh, God…" Her head rolled back. She was close. He knew the signs. That moment when her breathing became erratic and her hands flopped at her sides because she couldn't seem to control them.

He loved everything about her. Every inch of her body, mind, and soul.

Finally, her pussy clamped down on his cock, milking him as she rode the waves of her orgasm. He watched her, holding his breath, letting himself follow her over the edge seconds after her orgasm was complete.

Spent and satisfied, he eased out of her. "Don't move, hon." He tugged his jeans over his hips and padded over to the sink to get a wet washcloth so he could clean her up.

She watched him, a goofy, satisfied grin on her face. "You take such good care of me."

"It's my job."

She rolled her eyes. "Is this what my father's paying you for?"

He shuddered. That situation worried him, and he didn't need to be reminded. There was no telling what Secretary Loughlin was going to do when he found out about Tavis.

Shaking thoughts of her father from his head, he set his hands on her belly again. She did too, her palms on top of his. Their eyes locked, and they stared at each other.

Suddenly, her stomach moved.

Colette gasped, but so did Tavis.

"Did the baby just kick?"

Colette shifted her hands to find a spot to feel herself directly, though it was hard for her to squeeze her palms in between his, and he wasn't willing to give up this front-row seat to the baby moving.

And then it kicked again. Tavis grinned wide. "Oh, my God. That's so fucking amazing."

Colette giggled. "It feels so weird."

Another kick made them both chuckle. "He's going to be a linebacker."

"My kid is not playing football. Stop it. Besides, maybe it's a girl, and she's going to be a trapeze artist."

Tavis shook his head. "No kid of mine is going to swing up in the air doing death-defying acts."

Colette giggled and then grew serious. "There's a baby inside me."

It was suddenly far more real. "Yes. Apparently there is. I think I'm in love with him or her already," Tavis informed her.

She smiled at him, not saying a word.

He was pretty certain he had her convinced she was his forever, but he still had his doubts on occasion and he worried about what might happen when they got home. He worried about that often.

"We should get to campus," she murmured.

"Yeah." He helped her sit and then handed her her bra while he found her panties and jeans. He never took his eyes off her though. He loved the way her body was changing. He knew she was self-conscious about it, but he thought she'd never been sexier. She grew more appealing with every passing week.

They weren't late. Not even close. He had her on campus and in her lab with plenty of time to spare. When she was settled, he took a seat outside on his usual bench where he most often waited for her.

It had been five months, so many of her classmates knew by now that Tavis wasn't just her boyfriend but also her bodyguard. No boyfriend spent as much time as he did following someone around. That ship had sailed, but no one seemed to care.

He could see where it might have been annoying for her in the past to have her classmates hitting on her bodyguards, but since Tavis had been introduced first as her boyfriend, no one tried to steal him. He knew that pleased her.

When it was time for her to come out of the lab, he started paying closer attention. This was his usual routine. He never took his eyes off her if he could avoid it. Though not one thing had happened in the past five months to give him cause to believe her life was in danger, he was still being paid to protect her, and he didn't give a fuck about the money. He was in love with her. He would move mountains to protect her.

Someone kept occasional tabs on Steve Lacoste, but the man was still working for the same diplomat in Ethiopia, so Tavis had checked him off the list of people to be concerned about.

As for Richard Tillerman, for some mysterious reason, he'd stopped texting. Cold turkey. Suddenly, one day went by and then two and three and four and so on until it had been a week without a single text. And then a month. And then two.

Tavis hadn't known what to make of that situation. What had caused Tillerman to stop harassing her? It worried him, but he also counted his blessings. Ryker and Ajax kept half an eye on Tillerman. The man came and went from the bank where he worked with his father. He went on dates. He played tennis with his college roommate. He played golf with clients.

He did not continue to blackmail Colette.

A few students came out of the lab and headed to the left.

Tavis leaned back on the park bench, anxious to have Colette in his sight and then his arms. This damn lab was the most unnerving of her classes for some reason. He suspected it was because it was the place she went for the longest stretches of time. He grew antsy when he couldn't set his eyes on her for several hours.

He never went inside the lab. For one thing, it would cause a disturbance because technically only trained lab techs were permitted inside. Tavis could have worked around that rule of course, if he wanted to, but he made Colette nervous when he hovered.

Plus, the lab only had the one exit. She couldn't exactly escape him since he was watching the door.

Several seconds later, Colette stepped out, followed by Isaac Sorter. Isaac must have called to her because she turned to face him, smiling politely.

Tavis chuckled. Isaac often stopped to talk to Colette. The guy was relentless and unwavering, and he always glanced in Tavis's direction as if he were hoping one day she might break up with Tavis and decide to go out with Isaac.

It should have been annoying, but Isaac was not even close to being competition for Tavis, so Tavis forced himself to keep his blood pressure in check every time the foolish man shamelessly wasted his time flirting.

"Hey there."

The female voice caused Tavis to glance to the left to find two college girls coming toward him. They were probably freshmen. He figured eighteen or nineteen, twenty years younger than him, but they were geared up to shamelessly flirt with Tavis.

He rolled his eyes and glanced back toward Colette who was still talking to Isaac.

"We've seen you hanging around here a lot, but you never show up at any parties."

He snickered, trying not to be rude as he turned toward them again. "I'm a bit old for you two."

The brunette giggled and waved a hand around

dismissively. "Age is just a number." Her gaze roamed up and down his body as if he were eye candy ready to be displayed for nude sketches in the art department.

Another glance at Colette. She was nodding at something Isaac said. Isaac glanced at Tavis. He always did. Tavis wondered if the man would be just as relentless if he knew Colette was five months pregnant.

The brunette, who was apparently the spokesperson in this let's-see-if-we-can-get-the-hot-older-guy-to-go-out-with-us party of two, held up her phone. "Take a selfie with us."

He frowned. "Uh, no."

"Oh, come on. Be a sport. We're from Wisconsin. Studying abroad this semester. I'd love to be able to tell my friends back home that I dated this hot guy from South Africa while I was here." Her face lit up. "I'll tell them you were a professor."

He narrowed his gaze again. "I'm not a professor, and I'm not from South Africa," he pointed out needlessly. *Why am I engaging these two?*

"Of course. But no one will be able to tell that from a picture." She gave him a ridiculous pouty face. "Please."

"Not a chance." He jerked his attention back toward the lab. *"Fuck."* Tavis started jogging in that direction. Colette was gone. Nowhere in sight. He scanned the entire area as he hurried toward the lab.

Please God, tell me she went back inside for something.

Two more students were coming out as he approached. "Where's Colette?" he asked them as he pulled the door open and looked inside the room.

The taller man frowned. "She left a few minutes before us."

Tavis spun around. No Colette anywhere. No Isaac Sorter either. *Son of a bitch.*

There had to be a logical explanation, but the hairs on the back of his neck were standing on end as he jogged in the opposite direction from where he'd come. There was no way Colette had walked toward him or past him. He hadn't taken his eyes off her for more than a few seconds.

Heart racing, he tugged on the door of the closest building. It was locked. *Dammit.* He raced to the next one. Also locked. *Motherfucker.*

Think. Think think think. He searched the area. She couldn't have gone far. She could only be seconds away from him. Even if she were running, which wasn't something she did, and she certainly didn't move that fast now that she was five months pregnant.

The next building looked like more of a storage room for supplies or electrical equipment. It had no windows. Tavis wasn't going to leave any stone unturned. He dashed toward it and grabbed the door handle. It opened.

The moment he swung it wide, he heard her. It was a faint muffled scream of distress, and it tore at his soul. If someone hurt her…

Tavis pulled his weapon from its holster at his side and raced toward her voice, unable to see her yet.

"What the fuck? You're pregnant?" This voice was Isaac's. *Motherfucking fuck.*

Tavis considered strangling that piece of shit with his bare hands when he got to them.

From Colette came nothing more than a whimper, and Tavis realized why a second later when he rounded the corner of shelves piled with stacks of boxes. Isaac had one hand plastered over Colette's mouth and one hand on her stomach, pressing against it far too hard for Tavis's taste.

"Get your fucking hands off her," Tavis shouted as he lifted his gun. "Right fucking now, asshole."

Isaac spun around, but he took Colette with him, holding her in front of him as a human shield.

Colette's eyes were wide with fear and she screamed for a moment before Isaac covered her mouth again. He lifted his other hand to her neck. The guy held a long serrated knife against her tender skin.

The fury Tavis felt was indescribable and mixed with a certain amount of fear. But seriously, did this motherfucker think he could win a battle against Tavis?

"Do you have any idea who I am?" Tavis asked.

"How the hell do you have a gun on you?" Isaac responded. The guy's eyes were wide and he was trembling now. Good.

"Navy SEAL, jackass, and I've accurately shot dozens of men in the head in situations far more dire than this one to save a hostage. You want to take that chance or let her go?" He kept his voice level and even. It was his job.

Tavis had done this sort of thing more times than this asshole could count. This was not the same. Not even close. The hostage had never been his woman. But somehow Tavis managed to keep his cool.

"Shit," Isaac muttered. He only hesitated a second before releasing Colette and holding up his hands.

Colette gasped, her hand coming to her neck as she hurried toward Tavis.

He kept his gun raised, his gaze on Isaac as a commotion behind him alerted him more visitors had arrived.

"Campus police. What's going on?"

Tavis didn't need to turn around to recognize that voice. It was David Strickland, head of campus police. The man was six five and built like a truck.

Tavis knew every single person who worked for campus police. They knew him too. After all, he was the personal bodyguard for the secretary of state's daughter. Tavis had made a point of checking in with security at least once a week to make sure there were no rumblings of a threat against her.

David and two other men marched straight toward Isaac, whose eyes were wide as he looked around. "What the fuck, man? I didn't do anything."

David chuckled, his dark eyes dancing with mirth as he flipped Isaac around and flattened him to the wall. In seconds, Isaac was cuffed. He continued to grumble about it not being a crime to ask a girl out. He even argued that he'd simply been protecting her from Tavis.

David and his men said very little as they manhandled Isaac and removed him from the building.

Tavis kept a hand on Colette at all times, mostly shielding her behind his back. His heart was beating out of his chest as he waited for Isaac to be removed from her sight.

Finally, Isaac was out of the building. The only people left were two more police officers who had arrived a few seconds after the first three.

Tavis spun around, grabbed her shoulders, and let his gaze roam up and down her frame. He tipped her head back, relieved to see that she hadn't been cut. After verifying she wasn't bleeding, his hand came to her belly.

"I'm okay, Tavis," she whispered. She was shaking, but she didn't appear to be injured.

"He had his hands on you," Tavis growled, unable to contain his fury now that the immediate threat was gone. "I fucking glanced away and you were gone."

She grabbed his waist and stepped closer. "I'm fine."

He shook his head as he pulled her against his chest, threading his fingers in her hair and palming the back of her head to hold her tight. "This is my fault."

"It's not," she mumbled against his pecs. Her arms came around him. "It happened so fast. You're here now. I'm okay," she repeated.

He held her tighter, kissing the top of her head, not caring that two police officers were watching this exchange.

Colette shoved against him and tipped her head back when he gave her an inch. She cupped his face. "I never once picked up on the fact that Isaac could be a danger. He seemed like a nerdy college student to me."

"Me too, hon." Tavis took a deep breath. "My focus was on so many people who could have been a threat. He never entered my mind." He searched her face, looking for signs of distress.

She was shaking still but didn't look like she might panic. "Let's get out of here."

CHAPTER 21

Three weeks later...

"Do you really think this is necessary?" Colette asked as Tavis zipped up her suitcase. "I have one week of classes left. Surely we could stay one more week." She bit her lower lip, knowing this argument was moot. They were leaving today. Tavis insisted.

After the incident with Isaac, Tavis had managed to talk her dad off the ledge and buy her three more weeks, but he didn't like the idea of traveling on their originally scheduled flight. If anyone was paying attention and thought they might be able to ambush her at the airport, they would be a week late.

Colette leaned against the wall next to the door. Not only had Tavis insisted they go back to the States a week early, but he'd done every damn thing to make it happen. He'd spoken to her professors. He'd packed her things. He'd changed their flights. He'd also still cooked for her and fed her and even washed her body in the shower.

The man loved to take care of her, and usually she let him because she enjoyed it and she was so damn tired all the time.

"I don't see why this is necessary," she repeated, grumbling. She didn't really care about missing one week of classes. It was fine. But she had no interest in facing her parents. She would gladly put that off for another ten years. Maybe if they showed up with a ten-year-old child, her parents wouldn't lose their shit.

"Colette..." Tavis warned in his stern voice as he entered the bathroom, probably to make sure they had everything for the tenth time. His bathroom hadn't been used in months. Nor had his bedroom. Everything he owned was in here with her stuff.

"You said yourself the threat is over. Isaac was deported. He's in custody back in the States. He wasn't working with anyone. No one is going to bother me."

Tavis finally came to her. He was smiling as he met her gaze, flattened his body to hers, gripped her shoulders, and kissed her. "We're leaving, hon. I know you're nervous about facing your parents, but that's not going to change in a week. Time to rip the Band-Aid off. I'll be by your side every second. In front of you if need be."

She sighed.

He slid his hands down her arms and settled them on her belly, stroking the bump she wouldn't be able to hide from her parents. She'd suddenly expanded in the last few weeks. She knew they were living on borrowed time already. It was a wonder news of her pregnancy hadn't gotten out yet.

Tavis's expression was serious. "I need to say something and I want you to listen."

"Okay." She was nervous now. Was he going to break up with her or something?

He held her gaze. "This baby is mine, got it?"

She frowned. What was he talking about?

"It was irresponsible and unprofessional of me, but I fell hard for you the moment you arrived in Uganda. We entered into a relationship immediately and I was careless and you got pregnant."

Her eyes widened. *Holy shit.* He was so not breaking up with her. But… She couldn't let him do this. She shook her head. "Tavis…"

He squatted in front of her, kissing her belly as she held his shoulders. "Mine. My child. Understood?"

A tear slid down her face. "You don't have to do that. I'm a big girl. I can tell my parents I acted recklessly and had sex with a stranger. There's no need for you to take the heat." Her heart was thumping though. Love filled her chest, tightening it. Tavis would do that for her?

He rose to his feet again, but his hands were still on her baby bump. He ignored her arguments. "When you give birth, my name goes on the birth certificate. Got it? Not one single person alive ever needs to know differently. When the kid is older, if you want to tell him or her, we can discuss it then, but not for many years. This is my baby. I will love it as much as I love its mother." He cupped her face now and kissed her tear-streaked cheeks.

She sucked back a sob. "What about Joseph Rhineheart's family?" she whispered. She'd thought about them from time to time. They deserved to know they had a grandchild, a niece, a nephew, cousin…

Tavis smiled. "I had Ryker look into that. Turns out Joseph came out of the foster care system. He has no known family. The parents who were listed on the funeral notice were not his. They were simply the last foster parents he'd lived with."

Colette gasped. *Holy shit*. She swallowed hard, staring at Tavis. Could she agree to this proposition?

He lifted a brow. "There are no holes in our story, hon. None. Not a single one."

He was right. With the exception of blood types and future DNA issues if the child got sick, but no holes they needed to be concerned with in the immediate future. Her lip was trembling. "Why would you do this?"

"Because I love you more than life, and I want to be the bad guy here. It will save face in your family. It will keep the gossip to a minimum. So what if you got pregnant before you got married to your fiancé? That won't be newsworthy for very long. Sure, the guy is just a Navy SEAL, not a wealthy banker or political diplomat, and he doesn't have a doctorate in epidemiology." Tavis chuckled. "But you could do worse."

She blinked at him. She hadn't heard much after the word fiancé. "Tavis?"

"Oh, shit. I did that out of order." He chuckled again as he reached for his pocket and pulled out a small jewelry box. His hand was actually trembling as he held it out.

She couldn't breathe.

Tavis dropped to one knee and opened the box. "Colette Loughlin, will you do me the honor of being my wife?"

More tears fell. Why was she always crying? Her hand was shaking more than his as she held it out. "Yes," she managed before she started crying harder.

Tavis removed the enormous diamond from the box and slid it onto her finger. It fit perfectly. Why wasn't she surprised?

He was back on his feet, holding her tight a second later. Hands cupping her face, he kissed her cheeks and then came to her lips. "I love you so much it hurts, Colette."

"I love you too, Tavis."

She melted as he kissed her, her legs almost giving out. But Tavis held her up. He always did.

～

"How is this going to work?" Colette asked six hours later when they were settled in their seats in first class, headed to Amsterdam. She held her hand in front of her for the millionth time. The diamond was huge. She had no idea what kind of money Tavis made, but surely not enough to afford this ring.

"How is what going to work, hon?" he asked as he took her hand and kissed her knuckles.

"Where are we going to live? What am I going to do since I can't finish my PhD? I have about a million questions." She wasn't kidding. Her brain was running in every direction.

He shook his head, his eyes dancing with mirth. Confounding man. He probably had an answer. He had an answer for everything.

"Silly woman. You are totally finishing your PhD. We'll head to Baltimore in a few weeks after the holidays. Move into a larger apartment or rent a house. You'll get back to classes and labs and long evenings in the library. I'll stay home as your kept man to hold down the fort. After the baby is born, I'll turn into stay-at-home dad extraordinaire for a while so you can finish your dissertation. It's not complicated." He grinned.

She stared at him, blinking. Yes, he did have all the answers. Except one. "And how the hell are we going to pay the bills? I get a small stipend, but not enough for three people, one of them needing diapers and formula. It will never work. I need to quit school and go with you back to

Indiana so you can work and I can get a job." She bit her lower lip, trying not to cry.

He shook his head again. "Nope. Turns out you didn't fall in love with a random bodyguard who lives paycheck to paycheck. I have money, hon."

Her eyes widened further. "Oh."

He lifted a hand and pushed her lower jaw to close her mouth, chuckling. "I spent seventeen years in the Navy. Most of that time I saved everything I made. Plus, I get my full retirement."

"Oh," she repeated, trying to wrap her head around this development. Part of her had never believed she could finish her PhD. She hadn't fully let go of the dream. She'd continued to pretend it would happen, kept up with her research, worked hard, all of that, but this news was…life-altering.

He leaned over the armrest and kissed her. "It's going to be fine. You like my spaghetti sauce, right?"

She chuckled. "You kind of lied about your cooking skills. You're a god in the kitchen. I never would have eaten so well while I was in Uganda without you. I haven't thanked you enough. Not to mention all the other things you do for me. I'm the luckiest woman alive." She grabbed his hand and brought it to her cheek.

He eased her head onto his shoulder and kissed her temple. "I know the next few days are going to be hard on you, but I'll do everything in my power to smooth the path."

"You already have. I'm humbled by what you've done for me." She lifted her face. "You're serious? You want to stay home with the baby while I finish my PhD?"

"Of course."

"I promise when I'm done we can go wherever you

want. I can find work anywhere there's a university, hospital, or even a lab."

"We'll cross that bridge when we come to it. For now, we have a plan. It's a solid plan."

If she kissed him again, would it start to annoy the people across the aisle? Oh, fuck it. Who cared?

∽

"She's here," Colette's mother shouted over her shoulder the moment she opened the front door to let Colette and Tavis in. "I can't believe you wouldn't let us pick you up at the airport, and..." Her voice trailed off.

Colette wasn't surprised. It took her mother a second to notice Tavis, but when she did, her eyes went wide and her jaw dropped. Mostly because Tavis had a possessive arm around her and his fingers were threaded with hers over her baby bump.

She backed up a step. "Come in," she murmured, her gaze on Colette's stomach. There were so many things to absorb in that one frame. The combined hands, the giant diamond ring, the obvious baby bump.

Seconds ticked by. Important ones. Seconds that would determine how the next hours were going to go.

"So nice to meet you, Mrs. Loughlin. I'm Tavis Neade." Tavis held out a hand.

"Carolyn Loughlin," her mother murmured as she accepted the handshake, her gaze still on Colette's belly. She blinked several times and then moved in closer and pulled Colette to her chest, hugging her tightly.

A huge weight lifted from Colette's shoulders. It had been a long time since her mother hugged her like this. Carolyn Loughlin wasn't usually very demonstrative.

As her mother released her, her father stepped into the foyer. His expression was serious, narrowed, his gaze taking in his pregnant daughter and then the man whose hand was now resting on Colette's shoulder.

"Tavis Neade," her fiancé stated as he leaned around her to extend a hand to her father. "So nice to finally meet you."

Colette held her breath as she watched her father silently shake Tavis's hand.

Tavis slid his other arm around her chest, hauling her in closer to him. Supporting and claiming her at the same time. "We obviously have a lot to explain."

"Obviously," her father finally stated. "Let's move to the living room."

Colette's mother looked nervous and concerned as she walked next to her husband, leading Tavis and Colette to the living room.

Tavis never released Colette. He didn't just hold her hand, he kept his arm around her waist. He guided her to a loveseat and settled her next to him, his hand going to her thigh. He staked his claim in every way, making it clear that he was damn serious about her.

She had thought she'd have been more nervous than this, but it was hard to stress too hard when Tavis had her.

"I've asked your daughter to marry me, and she said yes," Tavis stated to open the conversation.

Her father lowered into an armchair. "Apparently that was appropriate," he pointed out, glancing at her stomach.

"Yes," Tavis agreed. "We wanted to wait and tell you in person. I also want to assure you that your daughter's safety was always my top priority from the moment we met. In addition, the Holt Agency is transferring every dollar you paid for my services back to your account. My intentions where Colette is concerned are one hundred percent honorable. I don't want there to be any doubt in anyone's mind."

Colette watched her father as he rubbed his chin. Her mother had taken a seat in the other armchair. She sat with a rigid spine, her legs crossed, hands casually over her knee. It was a memorized posture. Her wide-eyed expression hinted at her true feelings.

"That won't be necessary," William Loughlin stated. "You protected my daughter. That's what I paid you to do. And we're extremely grateful you were there when that asshole tried to kidnap her. If you hadn't been, Lord knows what might have happened next. From what I'm hearing, Isaac Sorter isn't talking. No one knows what his intentions were. Ransom? Selling her to the highest bidder? We don't really know if he knew whose daughter she was."

Tavis nodded. "I'm sure you're shocked, and you'll need time to absorb everything, but there isn't much to say. We were careless. I take full responsibility. But the truth is I'm in love with your daughter, and I intend to spend my life ensuring she's the happiest person on Earth."

Carolyn Loughlin gasped, her hand coming to her mouth. Her eyes were teary. Her mother cleared her throat. "I can't believe you're getting married, and having a baby. I'm so happy for you."

The tightness in Colette's chest eased. "Thank you, Mom." She rubbed her belly as Tavis's hand came over hers.

Her mother suddenly stood. "Oh. Drinks. You must be thirsty. The cook prepared hors d'oeuvres too. Colette, would you help me get them from the kitchen?"

Colette glanced at Tavis. This had been bound to

happen, but she didn't like leaving him alone with her father.

He smiled, kissed her cheek, and whispered in her ear. "It's okay. Go."

She stood, nervously shaking. Her gaze shifted to her father. "Dad..."

He glared at her. "I'm not going to murder the man in my own living room, Colette."

That did very little to appease her, but she reluctantly followed her mother.

∼

Seconds ticked by before Secretary Loughlin cleared his throat, and what he said shocked Tavis. Tavis had considered a lot of possible scenarios, but not this one. "I'm a man with many resources at my fingertips, Mr. Neade. If you think for one minute I don't know more than you do about the last six months, you're mistaken."

Tavis nodded, unsure where Loughlin was going with this but not willing to interrupt.

"First of all, I know everything about you. I know what happened a year and a half ago in Ethiopia. I know the exact dollar amount in your bank account."

Tavis swallowed. He should have thought of that. Secretary Loughlin probably had all that information even before his daughter got on the plane to Uganda. He refused to let the man see him sweat, so he forced a trained casual expression.

"Second of all, you're probably not aware of what happened with Richard Tillerman."

Tavis stiffened, unable to school his expression any further. "I had my people follow him, but you're right, sir, I don't know why he stopped bothering Colette."

Loughlin snickered uncharacteristically. "My wife didn't like Richard. She thought something smelled bad, so she insisted I put some men on him, and I never ignore my wife's intuition." He lifted a brow.

Tavis nodded. He understood the silent lesson.

"Didn't take long for my people to overhear Tillerman bragging that he had compromising pictures of my daughter from the night before she left the States."

Tavis swallowed. *Fuck me.*

"The asshole was blackmailing her," Loughlin stated, his hands slapping down on the arms of the chair. "So, I paid him a little visit. He even had some of the pictures printed out. Didn't take me long to convince him it would be in his best interest to turn over every fucking photo to me, wipe his phone and computer of all evidence, and keep his fucking lips closed for the rest of eternity. It would be a devastating embarrassment to both himself and his father if the photos I have of *him* ever got out."

Tavis stifled a gasp.

Loughlin smirked. "Man can't keep his dick in his pants, and he's not careful about it."

Oh. Nice.

"You won't have a problem with him ever again."

"Thank you, sir. I don't know what to say." Tavis was truly shocked. Everything about this interaction was unexpected.

Loughlin glanced at the door, presumably to ensure the women weren't imminently returning. He leaned forward, elbows on his knees. "I saw the photos."

Tavis held his breath.

"You may have developed a fondness for Colette over time. Not surprising. She's a wonderful woman. But you weren't sleeping with my daughter from the moment she arrived," he pointed out.

Tavis didn't move a muscle.

"You're a good man, Tavis Neade. I feel lucky to have you as a son-in-law." He stood and held out a hand. "Welcome to the family."

Tavis stood also, his heart so full it might bust out of his chest. He shook Loughlin's hand firmly. "I love your daughter, sir," he pointed out to make sure the man didn't think he was simply being altruistic.

"I know you do." He nodded over his head toward the minibar. "I think we need a drink. You a scotch drinker, Neade?"

"On occasion, sir."

"Please. Call me Bill."

Tavis followed Bill toward the minibar. "If you don't mind me asking, why did you hire me or any other bodyguard in the first place? Did you have a specific threat that concerned you?" This question had never been answered and had bothered Tavis from day one.

Bill glanced at Tavis as he poured the scotch. "I've had dozens of threats over the years. I don't tell Colette the specifics to avoid sending her into an unnecessary panic."

"I can understand that." Tavis took the offered glass from Bill's hand.

Bill smirked. "My daughter has always thought I was overprotective, but there has been more than one instance when a potential threat has been removed without her knowledge. People find out who she is and think they can make a buck extorting me." Bill took a sip of his scotch. "I'm sure Isaac Sorter was one such man. If it hadn't been for you, God knows what might have happened next." He lifted a brow.

Tavis understood completely. "I'll do everything in my power to ensure she is safe for the rest of her life. If I can't be close to her, I will make sure someone else is."

Bill drew in a deep breath. "I have no doubt you will, and my wife and I will sleep better knowing this." He held out his glass and Tavis clinked his against Bill's. This conversation had been beyond awkward and bizarre, but it had also gone far better than Tavis had expected.

CHAPTER 22

Six months later…

"My turn," Nancy Holt announced. "Give me that sweet baby." She reached out and took Sophia from Tavis's arms.

He smiled at Ryker and Ajax's foster mother. Mom to everyone in the room really. She was one of the best women he'd ever known in his life. Nevertheless, he liked to hold Sophia. She made his heart swell. Like her mother. He rarely handed her over to anyone.

Colette set a hand on his shoulder and rounded to face him. "I don't think Nancy is going to drop her, Tavis."

He nodded, forcing his brow to unfurrow. "I know that."

Colette chuckled and pulled him down to sit at the huge butcher block table in the Holt kitchen. This table had fed many a foster child over the years. It kept a lot of secrets too considering how many serious conversations had been had while seated around it.

The volume in the room was high since every

employee of the Holt Agency was currently on the farm. They weren't the only guests. Colette's parents were also in attendance. Her father had spent the afternoon riding around the land on horseback with Frank Holt, a man who was the only father figure Tavis had since his own parents were deceased. Ever since Tavis had joined the rest of his team in opening the Holt Agency, Frank had taken Tavis under his wing. So had Nancy. They were good people.

When Frank and Nancy had suggested Tavis and Colette hold their wedding on the farm, it had been a no-brainer. Colette hadn't wanted something flashy. She hadn't wanted the entire world to know. She'd wanted a simple wedding out of the public eye, and she'd bounced with excitement when the idea was presented six months ago when the two of them had come to visit before heading to Baltimore where Colette would finish her PhD.

"I can't get over how much this precious little gem looks like you, Tavis," Nancy cooed, never taking her eyes off Sophia as she cradled Tavis's angel in her arms.

Tavis smiled as Colette gripped his thigh under the table.

"She really does," Colette's mother agreed.

Tavis wasn't sure how much Carolyn Loughlin knew about Joseph Rhineheart, but he suspected nothing. Not even the name.

Tavis didn't need to glance at Secretary Loughlin to know the man would be subtly grinning. Tavis was biased of course, but he really did think Sophia looked like him.

"I'm not sure how I feel about this beard you've grown," Ajax joked from across the table. "I guess taking care of a baby night and day doesn't leave much time for shaving."

Colette tipped her head back and gave his beard a tug. "I like it."

"Of course you do," Serena agreed, swatting playfully at her husband. "It's sexy."

Ajax's eyes went wide.

Serena rolled her eyes. "Don't get your feathers in a ruffle, big guy. Your smooth face is sexy too."

Laughs erupted around the table.

"I can't believe you're getting married tomorrow," Xena exclaimed, clapping her hands together. She and Ryker lived here on the farm, and she'd taken on the task of helping with all the wedding arrangements, mostly through Tavis while Colette was buried in her studies.

Colette would smile sweetly at Tavis every time he came to her with a question about the wedding and say, "You know I don't care. Whatever you want is fine. As long as you're the groom, our friends and families are there, and the paparazzi can't get on the property, I'll be the happiest woman alive."

Damn, he loved her. He couldn't stop staring at her sitting next to him. His heart was full. His entire team was seated around the table. Keene, Larson, Heath, Kenner, Holden... Their given names anyway. He knew them all as Gramps, Keebler, Pitbull, Viper, and Loki. Ryker and Ajax rounded out the eight of them. Trek and Birdman. Grant had also joined the Holt Agency, but he was deep in an assignment and living in D.C. with his wife, Caroline, so he hadn't been able to attend.

Tavis was blessed beyond his imagination. So truly blessed.

∼

The wedding had been perfect. Not a single glitch. Colette was the most beautiful bride Tavis had ever seen. She was glowing as he watched her make her way around the room, ensuring she personally greeted every single guest and made them feel welcome.

Colette's mother was holding Sophia who wore a gorgeous fluffy dress that was nearly a replica of her mother's. It had been an extravagance Tavis had insisted upon. He'd wanted his daughter to make the entire room ooh and ah over her.

He couldn't wipe the grin off his face as Ajax joined him where he leaned against the wall. He was soaking in the room, committing this day to his memory. These people who were his family and closest friends.

Now that Colette had finished school, they would be moving here to the farm. Turned out she loved it here. The Holts had offered them a piece of their land to build a house on. Ryker and Ajax lived on this land too. It was so peaceful. Relaxing. Nothing like the bustling city that Colette hated. She was anxious to kick public life to the curb.

Colette would be working for a private medical company, most of which she could do from home for now. Tavis hadn't gone back to work yet. He was taking his time. Enjoying every moment of Sophia's life. That sweet cherub owned his heart. She truly did.

Ajax chuckled.

"What are you laughing about?" Tavis asked Ajax.

Ajax shook his head, still grinning. He glanced around, perhaps making sure no one else was in earshot. "Just thinking about Sophia. I'm a bit surprised is all. Wondering how you've managed to pull the wool over so many people's eyes."

"Don't know what you're talking about, Birdman." He kept his face straight.

Ajax narrowed his eyes, smirking. "I don't buy for one moment that you fathered that baby."

Tavis lifted his brows. "No idea what you mean. My name's on the birth certificate. You're pretty good with math. Checks out just fine."

Ajax shook his head slowly. "I know you, Bones. I'm not shocked you fell head over heels in love with Colette. She's fucking amazing. But I know you didn't sleep with her the night you picked her up at the airport." He glanced around again and spoke his next words at a mere whisper. "Good thing Joseph Rhineheart looked a lot like you."

Tavis simply shrugged and clapped a hand on Birdman's shoulder. "I wouldn't spread that story around. You'll sound loony."

Ajax made a motion to zip his lips. "You're a good man, Bones. One of the best."

"I love that woman and that baby more than life. They're both mine."

"I can see that." Birdman tugged Tavis in for a man hug and then let him go. "Lucky bastard."

"I sure am." Tavis found Colette's gaze across the crowded room and grinned from ear to ear as he headed toward her. He needed to touch her again. Remind himself she was his. Thread their fingers together. Hell, he needed this silly reception to be over so he could haul her to their hotel and ravage her sexy body all night long.

Her parents were staying with Frank and Nancy Holt for another day, enjoying the relaxation of life on a farm while babysitting their grandchild.

Tavis had tried to talk Colette into a week in the Caribbean or some other warm, relaxing spot, but she'd turned down every suggestion. He couldn't blame her. Sophia was wrapped as tightly around her finger as his. There would be plenty of time in the future for honeymooning. Right now, neither of them wanted to risk missing a milestone. What if Sophia cooed in a new tone or smiled crookedly or crawled or something and they missed it?

Nope. One night was all they were going to take for now, and Tavis intended to make sure they returned completely exhausted tomorrow.

It was time to get out of here. He wrapped his arms around his wife and pulled her into his chest, loving the way she fit there now that the baby was no longer between them. "Mrs. Neade, it's time to go. Say goodbye."

She giggled. "Okay." She rose up on tiptoes and kissed him. "I love you."

"I love you too. And I want to show you how much. If we don't get out of here in the next five minutes, I can't promise I won't start showing you in front of an audience."

She giggled again and hugged him tight.

God, he loved the feel of her arms around him. He closed his eyes and took a deep breath. His world couldn't be more perfect.

AUTHOR'S NOTE

I hope you've enjoyed this first book in the Holt Agency series. KaLyn Cooper and I are so excited to give all the rescued SEALs from our Shadow SEALs books their own stories. Are you ready for more?

> Rescued
> Unchained
> Protected
> Liberated
> Defended
> Unrestrained

ALSO BY BECCA JAMESON

Blossom Ridge:

Starting Over

Finding Peace

Building Trust

Feeling Brave

Embracing Joy

Accepting Love

The Wanderers:

Sanctuary

Refuge

Harbor

Shelter

Hideout

Haven

Surrender:

Raising Lucy

Teaching Abby

Leaving Roman

Choosing Kellen

Pleasing Josie

Honoring Hudson

Nurturing Britney

Charming Colton

Convincing Leah

Rewarding Avery

Surrender Box Set One

Surrender Box Set Two

Surrender Box Set Three

Open Skies:

Layover

Redeye

Nonstop

Standby

Takeoff

Jetway

Open Skies Box Set One

Open Skies Box Set Two

Shadow SEALs:

Shadow in the Desert

Shadow in the Darkness

Holt Agency:

Rescued

Protected

Defended

Delta Team Three (Special Forces: Operation Alpha):

Destiny's Delta

Canyon Springs:

Caleb's Mate

Hunter's Mate

Corked and Tapped:
Volume One: Friday Night
Volume Two: Company Party
Volume Three: The Holidays

Project DEEP:
Reviving Emily
Reviving Trish
Reviving Dade
Reviving Zeke
Reviving Graham
Reviving Bianca
Reviving Olivia
Project DEEP Box Set One
Project DEEP Box Set Two

SEALs in Paradise:
Hot SEAL, Red Wine
Hot SEAL, Australian Nights
Hot SEAL, Cold Feet
Hot SEAL, April's Fool
Hot SEAL, Brown-Eyed Girl

Dark Falls:
Dark Nightmares

Club Zodiac:
Training Sasha
Obeying Rowen
Collaring Brooke

Mastering Rayne
Trusting Aaron
Claiming London
Sharing Charlotte
Taming Rex
Tempting Elizabeth
Club Zodiac Box Set One
Club Zodiac Box Set Two
Club Zodiac Box Set Three

The Art of Kink:

Pose
Paint
Sculpt

Arcadian Bears:

Grizzly Mountain
Grizzly Beginning
Grizzly Secret
Grizzly Promise
Grizzly Survival
Grizzly Perfection
Arcadian Bears Box Set One
Arcadian Bears Box Set Two

Sleeper SEALs:

Saving Zola

Spring Training:

Catching Zia

Catching Lily

Catching Ava

Spring Training Box Set

The Underground series:

Force

Clinch

Guard

Submit

Thrust

Torque

The Underground Box Set One

The Underground Box Set Two

Wolf Masters series:

Kara's Wolves

Lindsey's Wolves

Jessica's Wolves

Alyssa's Wolves

Tessa's Wolf

Rebecca's Wolves

Melinda's Wolves

Laurie's Wolves

Amanda's Wolves

Sharon's Wolves

Wolf Masters Box Set One

Wolf Masters Box Set Two

Claiming Her series:

The Rules

The Game

The Prize

Claiming Her Box Set

Emergence series:

Bound to be Taken

Bound to be Tamed

Bound to be Tested

Bound to be Tempted

Emergence Box Set

The Fight Club series:

Come

Perv

Need

Hers

Want

Lust

The Fight Club Box Set One

The Fight Club Box Set Two

Wolf Gatherings series:

Tarnished

Dominated

Completed

Redeemed

Abandoned

Betrayed

Wolf Gatherings Box Set One

Wolf Gathering Box Set Two

Durham Wolves series:

Rescue in the Smokies

Fire in the Smokies

Freedom in the Smokies

Durham Wolves Box Set

Stand Alone Books:

Blind with Love

Guarding the Truth

Out of the Smoke

Abducting His Mate

Wolf Trinity

Frostbitten

A Princess for Cale/A Princess for Cain

ABOUT THE AUTHOR

Becca Jameson is a USA Today best-selling author of over 100 books. She is well-known for her Wolf Masters series, her Fight Club series, and her Surrender series. She currently lives in Houston, Texas, with her husband and her Goldendoodle. Two grown kids pop in every once in a while too! She is loving this journey and has dabbled in a variety of genres, including paranormal, sports romance, military, and BDSM.

A total night owl, Becca writes late at night, sequestering herself in her office with a glass of red wine and a bar of dark chocolate, her fingers flying across the keyboard as her characters weave their own stories.

During the day--which never starts before ten in the morning!--she can be found jogging, running errands, or reading in her favorite hammock chair!

...*where Alphas dominate...*

Becca's Newsletter Sign-up

Join my Facebook fan group, Becca's Bibliomaniacs, for the most up-to-date information, random excerpts while I work, giveaways, and fun release parties!

Facebook Fan Group:
Becca's Bibliomaniacs

Contact Becca:

www.beccajameson.com
beccajameson4@aol.com

- facebook.com/becca.jameson.18
- twitter.com/beccajameson
- instagram.com/becca.jameson
- bookbub.com/authors/becca-jameson
- goodreads.com/beccajameson
- amazon.com/author/beccajameson